DELIVERANCE
IN THE DARK

Deliverance in the Dark

BY

L. M. Blade

© 2022 by L. M. Blade

All rights reserved. This book or any portion thereof may not be reproduced or used in any manner whatsoever without the express written permission of the publisher except for the use of brief quotations in a book review.

ISBN: 9798784172440 (paperback)

To Grandma Amna, the greatest storyteller I have ever known.

Chapter 1

Happily Ever After

My greatest idea came to me while I lay dying. As the world around me blurred, as medics rushed in and out of focus, their voices muffling in their rush against time to stop the blood gushing from the gaping wounds on my arms, as my breathing turned shallow, all I could do was stare past their shoulders and smile.

The fluorescent lights of the hospital shone on me like distant stars in the cosmos. I envisioned an anthropomorphic Sun, so vibrant in his disposition, speaking to his beloved, the much more aloof Pluto: "Why, dear, we are so different, you and me. I burn eternally for you, but you are so cold! Why, my dear, sometimes I feel we are many worlds apart!"

I must have giggled at some point. I don't recall much of what was happening in the living world.

What I do recall was asking for my prized writing pen and laptop soon after regaining consciousness. I was handed my prized pen, my writing notebook, the journal in which I'm writing in now, and my laptop from home—what a sight

Franklin must have been at the reception area!—and the confused nurse gave me an overbed table I could set my laptop on so that I could work in bed. And there I sat, in my light blue hospital scrubs, IV line hooked to my arm. I began to type. One word. And then another. The words flew from my fingertips, and before I knew it, I was well into the first draft of what would become one of my most favorite books that I have ever penned.

I cackled with each cleverly constructed line. I punched the air with my fist when I came across the perfect word. The hospital staff must have thought I had lost my marbles. I did not care one iota. I had been so deep in the darkness just hours before, and now I was caught up in a whirlpool of euphoric escapism.

All I knew was to grab hold of this moment—my only lifesaver, the one thing keeping me (in)sane and alive, perhaps more so than the drugs pumping into my veins. It could also kill me, this hyperfocused obsession. Were it not for the kind staff, I might have forgotten to eat. My head spun, and my thoughts raced too fast for me to make sense of it all.

I sat, oblivious to the doctors and nurses who lined up to examine me and the monsters in my head, on the pinnacle of reality and the precipice of sanity. I was only vaguely aware of their questions as goosebumps began prickling my skin from my characters breathing down my neck, and I felt my body soar through the cosmos to meet them, to live their lives, abandoning my own.

Madly brilliant or brilliantly mad, I could tip over at any moment in either direction, into the throes of my greatest creative genius or into the deepest, darkest depths of a mental breakdown.

It wasn't the first time, nor would it be the last, I suspected.

But this episode was certainly among the worst.

And should anything happen to me, you are free to blame my demise on the United Domains.

* * *

Amber Valley, a district of Chicago, Midwestern Province • January 1, 892 NE

First day of the new year. A Monday. It was said that the first day of Year 1 of the New Era was marked when a human stepped out into the world and saw that the sunlight had graced Earth for the first time in hundreds, if not thousands, of years.

That day was snowy yet bright, so the first human had declared it a Sunday. And from then on, humans began counting the days once more, no longer afraid, no longer living in the dark.

The android AC-A893 smiled every time she recounted this tale. Humans, as she understood, held on to stories of their elusive past. These stories nourished them as much as the food they consumed. Stories offered comfort, wisdom, answers.

Her newest patient, based on the dossier she had been provided, also deeply valued stories, both histories and fictional works. And so AC-A893 had downloaded as much knowledge as she could into her database to prepare herself for their first meeting. She did not count herself an expert by any means; the information stored inside her wasn't of the same caliber as that in historian androids, but it would be sufficient to allow her to connect with her newest patient.

For the first morning of this new year, the community hospital appeared relatively calm and quiet.

"Expect a lot of admissions and emergencies from last night!" AC-A893's clinician had warned her prior to dispatch. "Heaven knows what could have gone wrong while everyone was out partying." Perhaps their district was just peaceful, because so far nothing AC-A893 had witnessed aligned with her clinician's warning.

AC-A893 roamed the halls. From her nondescript appearance, she looked like any other android. Nothing on her gave away from which facility she had been dispatched. She was a normal model of average human stature, her body white like the hospital walls. Her LED lights glowed a soft blue hue meant to calm even the most agitated human. Quite standard. A vintage-styled nurse's collar was the sole indication that she was a medic android.

AC-A893 stopped by at the nurses' station, bowing briefly in front of the humans and other androids. She held her wrist under the optical scanner and waited. A nearby computer beeped, and a nurse looked up.

"Oh, you are the android from—yes, we were expecting you," she said and jumped to her feet. "I assume you have all of the patient's medical records already downloaded?"

"For the patient in room 514? Yes, I do."

"Then you're all set."

The nurse led AC-A893 to a suite at the end of the hallway, motioned to the closed door, and gave a small wave as if bidding her a good day. Then, without another word, she left.

AC-A893 glanced around, wondering why her patient was placed here, tucked in a corner far from the nurses' station, when she had been marked as high risk.

Deciding it didn't matter for now, she gave the door a knock.

When no reply came, AC-A893 announced her arrival and pushed the door handle down.

Nothing could have prepared AC-A893 for the sight that greeted her.

Blue and purple magical light filled the room. Her patient sat in her bed, furiously typing away on a laptop perched on the overbed table. Nearby lay an open notebook, in which she scribbled from time to time, leaving magic symbols in her wake. Her eyes glowed a brilliant blue, so unnaturally vivid, as though they were cybernetic.

There was someone else in the room.

Are they floating? wondered AC-A893, noting the lack of feet on the ground. Immediately she snapped a photo through the lens of her eyes for future analysis. The being stood tall and was wrapped in a long, hooded cloak that looked like it was made of strips of old parchment paper blotted with ink. Swaths of thin golden thread bound their torso. Their face was a completely blank canvas, and they floated eerily a couple feet off the ground, hunching over the woman. Blue light surrounded the two as though they were silently conversing over the worktable.

The woman looked up, finally noticing AC-A893. The apparition disappeared, and the woman's eyes dimmed to a slightly less vivid shade of blue.

AC-A893 composed herself before speaking.

"Ms. Sadiyeh Al-Ghul?"

The light emanating from the laptop screen gave the woman's complexion a pale, ghostly look. The open notebook continued to exude magical wisps that seeped into the long, thick, dark curls of the woman's hair and disappeared.

Across from her, the wall television played on mute. It was set to the news channel, AC-A893 noted.

"Please," Sadiyeh greeted, "I prefer to go by my publishing name, Sadiyeh Mhalabiyeh. But you can just call me Sadiyeh."

"Of course."

AC-A893 nodded and filed the information away: Sadiyeh Mhalabiyeh. Twenty-eight years old. Admitted to the hospital on New Year's Eve after being found unconscious in her bedroom. A published author, known for her humor (rather ironic, given her own situation). Magi…that would explain the bright eyes and the symbols coming from the notebook. The android had only been in commission for a short number of months, but she had heard of the Moonchildren before. Sadiyeh would be her first official Moonchild patient.

She ran a quick linguistic analysis on "Sadiyeh Mhalabiyeh" and chuckled. "Your name does have a nice ring to it. It rhymes."

Sadiyeh's face lit up with her grin. "That's why I picked it. A name like that on the cover should inform any prospective reader of what sort of wit to expect before they even turn to the first page. And *mhalabiyeh* is delicious!"

The android offered a smile, because she knew that displaying warmth would help her establish a relationship with the patient. Her search database pulled up an image of *mhalabiyeh*. "I am viewing an image of this dish. It does seem appetizing."

Sadiyeh's blue eyes took on a longing, morose gaze. "Oh, yes. Warm, fragrant milk pudding, a bit of rice if you wish, a dash of mastic, any toppings you desire—pistachios and raisins for me. My favorite dessert growing up, even during my moments of...*well*—Brian and the others were quick learners! They had hundreds of years to practice all sorts of cuisines from around the world! My mothers weren't around, but Brian wanted me to have the full experience of my culture, so…"

She gave an awkward shrug.

"And your first name, Sadiyeh. If you do not mind me commenting, it is such a lovely name. My database tells me it is Arabic in origin, and that it means good luck and happiness."

Sadiyeh's laugh, which sounded rather hollow to AC-A893's ears, only highlighted the shadows under her eyes. "Destined for happiness—I wish! Behind every step in the adventures of my stories I pen is me, on a perilous quest for happiness. At the very least, I do hope my readers find the joy I have been searching for! I am Sad, Sadness seeking Happiness—Oh! That would make a good book title someday…"

AC-A893 studied her patient carefully. She had seemed so fine while she was lost in her writing…

Giving an awkward cough, Sadiyeh stretched and shut her laptop. She glanced at AC-A893.

"So…state your purpose, Myla's Gift to Humankind," she said, referencing the founder of the androids during the first decade of the New Era. "I sense that something is different about you from the other medic androids."

AC-A893 nodded. "You sense correctly. I was sent by the Cognitive and Behavioral Health Clinic to take on your case."

"Ah, of course! I was told I was getting an android friend. So, this is going to be a long-term relationship."

"Yes, ma'am."

"At least you weren't sent by the United Domains."

Why would the global government wish to send an android to a Moonchild? AC-A893 wondered briefly, and then shrugged off the comment. Perhaps it was just Sadiyeh's sense of humor at play.

"What's your name?" Sadiyeh asked.

"We go by our model and serial numbers within the clinic. I am model AC-A893, serial number 419-NH0-5015-88."

"You expect me to memorize all that?!"

"We purposely do not have a name so that our client may assign us one in addition to pronoun usage. Additionally, we each come with a limited setting in terms of appearance, as we do not have an outer fleshy layer reminiscent of human skin, as you can see. But you may alter the color of my irises and some features of my nasal structure, mouth, eyebrows, and cheekbones."

"I like you the way you are," Sadiyeh said. "As for a name… how about Midway? Apparently, there was a battle fought a long, long time ago during a period known as World War II. That battle was called the Battle of Midway. They named an airport after it here, long before that place became the Midway Central Monorail Station."

"Midway," AC-A893 echoed, and then registered the name into her central storage. She was now Midway. "You enjoy reading up on the Old Era history of Chicago?"

Sadiyeh nodded. "I do. And I'd like for you to meet me midway in my recovery."

Sadiyeh and Midway chuckled in unison. A writer's specialty: choosing a name with multiple meanings.

"I hope to achieve that during our time together." Midway took another bow. "Of course, you are aware why I was sent to meet you."

A soft sigh escaped Sadiyeh's lips. She stared up at the ceiling, hands folded above her stomach.

"Yep," she said bluntly.

She's closing up on me, Midway thought. "Are you not ready to talk? I understand that I may have been dispatched a bit prematurely—"

"You're fine," Sadiyeh said, her voice strangely flat, no longer carrying the playful tone from before. Guarded. "It's just… how do I begin?"

Midway produced a small tablet from the compartment inside her torso and flipped through the notes. "According to what a Brian from your household told our staff, you were found beside your notes with your wrists split open."

"Not my brightest moment," Sadiyeh said, smiling darkly. "Hope I didn't bleed too much on those notes. I hate having to try to retrieve lost prose or character sketches. Those can take forever!"

"Why, Sadiyeh? Were you in pain? Did something hurt you?"

Sadiyeh continued to stare at the ceiling in silence. Midway stood patiently, tablet in hand. She could stay in that stance forever if she needed to—unless the clinic or Sadiyeh herself dismissed her.

Every now and again, Sadiyeh's gaze would stray to her laptop before she'd pull it away, avoiding Midway.

How curious, Midway thought. *Sadiyeh still has stories she wishes to tell.* But why, then, had she attempted to take her own life?

Just as Midway began weighing her options on probing Sadiyeh again, her patient spoke.

"Midway...can you prove that you exist?"

Sadiyeh's question was posed in a very low, soft, almost scared voice. Midway instinctively took a seat beside her patient, placing the tablet on her knees.

"Prove my existence?" Midway weighed the question. "I have already given you my model and serial numbers. I was booted into existence on the thirteenth of October 891 of the New Era under commission of the Cognitive—"

"That isn't what I meant," Sadiyeh said with a little chuckle. Then, more to herself, she pondered, "What could be the odds? We share the same birthday..."

She met Midway's gaze. "I mean...your consciousness. How do you know you're really...here? That you really exist? That you're not a lie, an illusion made up by someone else?"

Midway felt her internal drive whirl as it tried to process Sadiyeh's questions some more. "I...existence...do you mean... a soul, perhaps? Or something else? Consciousness? I suppose I do have thoughts, but then how else can an android process questions and requests from the humans they serve?

"I suppose what I am trying to say is...No, I cannot prove I truly exist, but I do know who made me and what purpose I serve. But whether I am real or not...I cannot tell you. I do not believe that is a question anyone can truly answer. But I certainly do feel real."

"Although some just see you as a walking, talking hunk of plastic?"

That took Midway by surprise. "Plastic? Well, I suppose if we were to each break down our forms into simpler matters, then at our most basic, we are nothing more than a collection of atoms without thought or emotions."

Sadiyeh chortled. "Then you, an android, just saw a glimpse of my thoughts when I decided to do away with myself."

"You questioned your existence?"

Sadiyeh didn't say anything for a little while. Then: "The Moonchildren are a mystery even now, nearly nine hundred years after we came out of the Era of Black Sun. Humans entered the New Era fully aware that there were those among us who had attributes and powers we couldn't explain easily with science. When we, the Moonchildren, emerged, there were proper names already hanging on our tongues. We already knew what we were called. We just didn't know *how* we existed or *why*. Just that we were a fact of life. We were treated with dignity like other humans. Our existence was respected.

"Magi, the humans gifted with magic; Lupinites, the werewolves; and Desmonites, the vampire bats. Those are the Moonchildren, the children of Sahariel, Desmoniel, and Dhibiniel. Where did these words come from? These names? What language did they originate from? We tried to trace the etymology, speculating that the names had changed over time from what they originally were. These names and words must have existed since the dawn of humankind.

"Every culture seemed to hold a ghost of the legend of our

kind. But, rather strangely, we couldn't find a singular unifying source.

"Yet we still had fragments of stories passed down from our ancestors during the Black Sun Era, stories they wanted to ensure survived that dark time. We knew that Sahariel, Desmoniel, and Dhibiniel were the Daughters of the Moon, and they were likely only three out of many more. We knew there was a Moon Mother, and across all cultures, across history, there are stories of a Moon Goddess.

"As you may have guessed, the Moon fascinated us. Does the Moon Mother still live there? Is the Moon where we originated from? We're human through and through, but the Moon is also a part of us, *somehow*. We became fascinated by her and what she could reveal about us, our past, and why we exist."

Sadiyeh paused to take a deep breath.

"Other humans also shared in our fascination with the Moon—and all of space. After all, we had been in the dark for so long, on the brink of extinction, alone. Our loneliness was why we made you, the androids, to accompany us as we got back on our feet.

"When we survived, when we flourished, we couldn't help but wonder: What if we weren't alone? What if the existence of the Moonchildren was a sign that there's more out there?

"So you can imagine our reaction when we discovered that our ancestors had been to space."

Midway recorded everything Sadiyeh said, nodding occasionally to show that she was listening. As Sadiyeh spoke, a smile blossomed across her face, and her expression was one of wistful contentment.

"The Age of Restoration ran from the 400s to the 600s of the New Era. That was when we began archaeological digs into our past and discovered and restored so much of the Old Era. This led to a fevered love for the old ways, and an obsession to express ourselves. The Age of Romance followed, when we as a race blossomed into a new spring after a long, grave winter. We expressed our uniqueness, all the while paying homage to our beloved past.

"They've been calling the last century the Age of Opulence. Some of the greatest minds in the sciences and the arts have come about since. We've been thriving in so many ways! And all because our ancestors have given us hopes, dreams—promises!

"That was when we first learned about space travel. The thought lingered, first as wishful thinking—we still had so much to take care of here, so much of the world still left to rebuild—but in the last twenty years, space was all anyone could think of! The Moonchildren were especially excited; what could we learn about space, about our heritage?

"But then—but then—" Her features shifted. "*That* happened. I questioned *everything*. I feared *everything*. I felt everything and nothing at once. I let the United Domains and their damned discovery get to my head. I let them crumble the walls around me, let them get to me, let them get to my wrists!"

"You keep mentioning the government—"

"Look! They're talking about it right now!"

Sadiyeh grabbed the remote and unmuted the TV. The sound of the news channel, where the broadcaster was interviewing a proclaimed science expert, blared across the hospital suite.

Midway was starting to see where the problem lay.

"The Moon landing..." she trailed off.

Sadiyeh nodded solemnly.

"They've been talking about this for weeks," Midway said.

"And worsening my state of mind every day," Sadiyeh said. "Listen, I've had my bouts of depression and dark thoughts before. I've struggled with them all my life. But I've been doing well in recent years. Outside of my writing career, I have a job. Some might find it boring, but I like it! I'm alone all day, punching in numbers for a lab; the androids I work with are more like the robots of old. It gives me time to sit there and think up new worlds and stories.

"I go to work. I come home and write my heart out until I pass out in bed. I'm never out of ideas. Either it's a book that'll be published later that year or that big, big project I'm working on, which began with these weird recurring dreams. I have a publisher. I have a number of books to my name. I am happy—or, rather, I *was* happy!

"But then I learned that humans had discovered that the first Moon landing was faked. In fact, we've never been to the Moon. We've never been to space. We're trapped here, forever."

Midway furrowed her brows as she concentrated on putting the pieces together. From the perspective of a Magi struggling to learn of their heritage in a tattered world with a shrouded past, this indeed was devastating news.

"I am sorry the news hit you so hard," Midway said. "Even if these achievements turned out to not be true back then, though, there's nothing to say they cannot become a reality now, correct?"

"*No!*" Sadiyeh said hotly. "The evidence found by the United Domains suggests that leaving the Earth's atmosphere exposes humans to insane amounts of radiation, meaning if you try to leave here, you're fried to ashes. So no luck *ever* trying to get to the Moon.

"Funny, though. We have records—video footage, even!—of the first Moon landing! All the evidence that says space travel was a reality! Yet they focus on one little piece that places everything into question?"

Radiation poisoning is a legitimate concern, thought Midway, who was, by design, concerned for the safety and well-being of humans. She had no doubt humans could figure a way out of this problem, but this was not the topic distressing her patient.

Sadiyeh went on, her face growing red. "*Now* they're saying it was all fabricated because of some political strife between nations of that period!"

"The human races of the Old Era were at war with one another for a long time," Midway said patiently. She hadn't been prepared to tackle heightened emotions over new discoveries, and she hoped her current setting was sufficient.

"I know that! And that would give a motive for fabricating this lie to feed the masses, to win some stupid vanity war with another country. But it's still strange! The timing of *this* news, the possibility of *this* being a political move in and of itself... Do you understand?"

Midway cocked her head to one side. "I don't believe I follow."

Sadiyeh bit her lower lip. "Maybe I've said too much. Nothing I say to you will reach anyone else's ears, will it?"

"The clinic has a strong policy on patient confidentiality. What you tell me will not be shared with the clinic or anyone else. I will only report that we have met, nothing more. But I am obliged to notify the clinic and hospital staff if you actively become a danger to yourself or others. I am here to offer an ear. Your medications are handled by a human expert."

Sadiyeh threw herself back on the hospital bed. "Good. Listen, something just feels off about the entire thing. I can't believe I'm about to confess this, but the thought has come up from time to time—I've heard those fears spoken from others, and honestly…it does make sense.

"This isn't the first time the United Domains have done something to harm the Moonchildren. It's been tiny little things adding up for many, many years now. I'm getting worried that they're trying to erase us."

Midway paused, unsure how to proceed. "Erase the Moonchildren? Out of existence?"

"Yes," Sadiyeh said. "Erase us…out of history, out of everyone's memories—remove us from this world. I don't know what they're planning or why, but the more they come out with laws or discoveries such as this, the more certain I become that they have their eyes set on eradicating us!

"Oh, I know how crazy I must sound! The United Domains shall make conspiracy theorists out of us all!"

Sadiyeh covered her face with her hands. Midway reached over and gently stroked her arm. "It's okay to be worried. There is so much uncertainty surrounding your people's past."

"And I know how unfounded this may sound," Sadiyeh continued. "One or two inconveniences, well…you can't have everything. But lately it seems like everything the United Domains do is at our expense. We are the ones to get ostracized and silenced every time. For the last hundred years or so, the Lupinites have found it harder to find jobs. There's nothing outright outlawing them, but nothing is protecting them either—after all the times Lupinites contributed to advancing the world! Unemployment rates, living below the poverty line...they've skyrocketed among the group. And then you have a growing misconceived perception that Lupinites carry diseases, like they can infect others with their condition. Put that all together and you have many who have ended up behind bars for possession of street drugs and the like. What did the United Domains expect would happen when the Lupinites have nothing else?

"And I don't know if you've heard what some Lupinites have been doing in retaliation, but it certainly isn't making the rest of us look better."

Midway straightened her back as Sadiyeh sat back up, staring at her laptop and notebook. The magic symbols had long since evaporated. As Midway processed her patient's words carefully, she studied the way the Magi rubbed her thumb over her laptop.

"And that's why you attempted to end your life?"

Sadiyeh nodded. "One bad thing too many, you know? I could endure everything else. We could endure a callous global government. At least there was the space program. We had something to look forward to. But then to be told there was nothing waiting for us beyond the stratosphere...

"No words can ever explain how empty, cold, and numb I

felt that week. The one last thing I was holding on to had been set ablaze. I couldn't bear to go on!

"I even began to speculate: What if we were mad after all? An ancient word for the Moon, *luna*, is also shared by the word lunatic. Maybe we *were* just mad. That's why I asked if you could prove your existence. Because no one can. No matter what evidence you have.

"If we go by the United Domains, we cannot trust even our own damn selves—ha! What's next? New York never existed? The Maldives? Will we learn that there was never an island known as Great Britain? That these places never submerged into the ocean because they never existed in the first place?"

"Sadiyeh…"

Sadiyeh hung her head, and her long curls curtained her face. A few moments later, she threw her head back and shook the hair away from her face, smiling ruefully.

"I'm glad you're here, Midway," she said. "You're like Muse, but someone I can speak to about something else."

"Muse?"

"You've seen them already," Sadiyeh said and motioned toward the laptop and notebook. Midway nodded, but something probed at her.

"Sadiyeh, are you alone?"

"Yes—well, not really, but…yeah. I'm okay with that."

"Who is Brian? He was the one who found you unconscious."

"He owns the manor I live in. Murklins Manor. Most of it is a hotel for…*well*."

"Do you rent a room at the manor?"

"Sort of…I mean, I've known Brian since I was a baby. But

I don't want to overstay my welcome, you know? It's hard to explain."

"And who is this Brian?"

"Like I said, Brian owns Murklins Manor. He's a butler—a skeleton butler, actually."

"Oh? You mean he was designed to look like a skeleton?"

Sadiyeh shook her head. "No, no! He's really a skeleton! Nothing but bones! He used to be a living human being during the Old Era. Murklins Manor is a hotel where the undead stay awhile or stop by for drinks."

"Oh." Midway had to process all that information. How could a skeleton think without a brain?

"And this Murklins Manor..."

"It's a refuge for the undead. My ancestors knew about this place. There are others like it, but we keep their existence secret. The dead don't want to be disturbed."

"Understood. You did mention a family beyond just your mothers."

"I write to my cousin. She's really young, but for a while I did live with her family. Not my thing, so I came back to the manor. I like being alone."

"Ah," Midway said. So Sadiyeh was mostly alone at work, her family was distant, and she seemed to keep to herself at the manor. An active social life didn't seem to be Sadiyeh's way. While introversion was perfectly fine, Midway felt that it would be best if she stayed with Sadiyeh at her residence for some time. But would Sadiyeh consent to this?

Sadiyeh was studying her laptop intently, deep in thought, when she let out a sudden snort. "Really dumb of me to try to end it all. I shouldn't have let the United Domains get to my head like that, but want to know something funny? I ended up having a great story idea. Of course, I'd never recommend that particular method of inspiration to anyone. Even though I tried to kill myself, I didn't want to die. Does anyone ever truly want to go? I just wanted the pain to stop."

"You were deep at work when I first came here," Midway observed.

"I was," Sadiyeh concurred with a giggle. She touched her laptop, and it was as though she had touched the Moon itself, for a small, comforted smile spread across her face. "I'm thinking of calling this book *Worlds Apart*. A bit of a simpler title than what I usually go for, but it will suffice. I suppose I've reached new heights of insanity, because when I was told that there's nothing waiting for us out there in space, I decided to give the celestial bodies a voice themselves.

"In my story, the Sun is in love with Pluto, but she is very cold and unreceptive to his advances. Cue a lot of cheesy planetary and temperature puns! Oh, but should I change it to Mercury instead of the Sun? I mean, Mercury has a diurnal temperature…that could be fun to play around with.

"And the ending! It's a wild and hilarious love story, but I want the characters to live happily ever after. Pluto has friends in Charon and her other moons. They could try to play matchmaker. Yeah…I think I will have Mercury involved somehow."

Midway offered a supportive smile. She had not been downloaded with any program to aid in artistic critique or creative thinking, but she wished to help her patient. "I'm afraid I cannot give advice on that, but you do seem to have a wonderful idea going!"

Sadiyeh beamed. "I...think I would like to bring Muse out again, if that's all right with you?"

Midway stood up and bowed. She watched as Sadiyeh took a pen from the spiral binding of her notebook and squeezed the grip. A shadowy figure materialized from the tip before re-forming into the tall ghostly figure from before, their robes parchment white and billowing as though they were standing outside on a breezy day. Faceless though Muse was, Sadiyeh smiled up at them as if meeting an old friend.

"I have some new ideas," Sadiyeh said. "Ready?"

Muse didn't reply, but the two inclined their heads together as if speaking in whispers, and with that Sadiyeh fell back into work.

Midway sent her status update to her clinic—*Met with patient*—and then filed away the entire encounter in her memory bank. She stood by and watched as Sadiyeh worked, content in her own tiny world, surrounded again by blue and purple light and magic symbols, unbothered by the demons of uncertainty from before.

Midway could not help but smile. This was her first patient who was both a Magi and a published author. She looked forward to working with her and seeing her new book come to fruition.

* * *

Downtown Chicago, Midwestern Province • March 15, 892 NE

"Absolutely not." Clive Gordon of OakFinch Press threw the manuscript back at Sadiyeh.

She stared at him in disbelief. "Why not?!"

This was the same man who had laughed until he turned blue in the face the first time he read one of her earliest manuscripts. "You're a mad genius!" he had said back then.

Now the portly man lifted off his bottle-thick glasses and rubbed one tired eye. "Listen, Mhalabiyeh. Every publishing company right now's got strict orders to not publish anything involving outer space."

"*Every* publishing company? That's outrageous! You can't silence art!"

Gordon lifted a hand, pleading for silence. "I know, I know. But this is out of my hands, I'm afraid. You know how much the public loves books and stories on outer space. Before the recent discovery, they were our top sellers—for the past two decades, in fact.

"But orders are orders. We believe if we stop selling content with space, the public will quietly focus on other subjects. We hope it will ease the heartbreak surrounding this news."

Heartbreak? So it wasn't just me hit by this news, Sadiyeh realized. The thought should have been comforting, but it only led to a mounting sense of unease.

Others feel that something's off about the whole thing too.

"Listen, we've noticed readers are getting into flowerpeople, if you would like to give us something with that."

Sadiyeh stared at her rejected manuscript as a cold feeling of dread ran up from her stomach to her throat. She had worked hard on the book for three months and, heeding Midway's advice, had barely listened to the news aside from whatever highlights Brian or someone else had shared. "Was this some sort of new law passed for all publishing houses?"

"Yes, it was. Back in mid-January."

"Who gave those orders?"

"The United Domains."

Chapter 2

Turning Point

Amber Valley • March 21, 893 NE

N₀ ONE COULD pinpoint exactly when in history the entire world fell into darkness. No records could indicate exactly when the Old Era ended and the Black Sun Era began. No accounts shed light on why or how this global catastrophe occurred, nor could they count the exact number of lives lost. Virtually none of the handwritten records that did survive into the new era could even begin to describe exactly what the Black Sun was. But every human since that moment dreaded returning to those dark days.

Sadiyeh shifted under her covers, her eyes shut tight.

All that was known was that when the Sun was seen at long last, the Earth's true Sun, relief and hope reverberated throughout the world. And as the world began anew, humans looked back through the darkness in hopes of retrieving what they could of their ancestors' past. They thirsted for knowledge of who they were, where they'd come from, tales of their cultures, their beliefs, their heritage.

But always, always, a little fear remained, a suspicion lingering in the back of every human mind, unspoken yet shared among all: Was there something they were supposed to remember? What sort of secrets had been left buried in the Black Sun Era? What sort of dangers, what sort of evils, were they not seeing before their very eyes?

"Sadiyeh?"

Sadiyeh moaned softly and opened her eyes. Midway stood at one corner of her bedroom beside the floor-to-ceiling window that took up nearly the entire width of the room. Bookcases lined the walls on either side of her doorway, save for an archway to the right, which led to a simple bathroom, and on the other side, a small alcove from which her bed stuck out. A little ways off near the window stood her writing desk.

"It is now four thirty in the morning," Midway reported. "You requested that I wake you at that time. Did you have a restful sleep?"

"Sorta," Sadiyeh replied. She hopped out of bed and checked her laptop, nibbling the hard-boiled egg Brian had left for her.

"How are you feeling?" Midway asked.

"Still about the same," Sadiyeh said, fetching her bath towels and heading for the shower. For a brief moment every morning, she would wake up feeling fine before she remembered that the United Domains so rudely existed.

Nevertheless, in the end, she had written another book for her publisher. On flowerpeople, just as Gordon had advised. *The Thorne in Rose's Side* was about a flowerperson named Rose and her messy relationship with the titular deuteragonist, both characters as forgettable and plain as the other. Sadiyeh had written that novella half-heartedly in about two weeks and soon afterward couldn't really recall what the story was about.

But she did recall this: after Gordon had finished editing her manuscript, right before the novella headed off to the printing press, Sadiyeh couldn't help but slip in one tiny line in which Rose and Thorne studied the night sky and fawned over the beauty of the Moon together.

It was just enough for her to be an ass, but not so much that she'd get her publishing company into trouble with the United Domains. At least Gordon hadn't seemed to notice.

The memory of that put a smile on Sadiyeh's face as she stepped out of the shower and brushed her teeth.

The book ended up selling well enough, but Sadiyeh suspected it was just because her name was on the cover. Whether her readers actually enjoyed the book was another matter. She never trusted what was said on the internet. Beyond the trips to and from work and the occasional meetings with her publisher, Sadiyeh seldom ventured out into the open, preferring the sanctuary of home and the tranquility of work, just her and the computers and numbers.

Gordon had praised her for listening to his advice, but little did he know that Sadiyeh was working on another book all along, titled *Uranus in Virgo*. She had shared her newest creation with Midway and Muse, unable to hold back fits of laughter over the risqué title.

"What could this possibly be about? Love of astronomical proportions? A heist across the cosmos?"

At Sadiyeh's behest, her aunt had consulted her thick tome on astrology over the phone. "Uranus is the planet of revolution, enlightenment, and radicalization, so when Uranus is in Virgo, it...Sadiyeh, are you paying attention?"

Sadiyeh grinned at that memory. Oh, how hard she had laughed! Everyone had thought she had stopped breathing! It was only too bad she could not publish either *Worlds Apart* or *Uranus in Virgo*.

After slipping into her work attire, Sadiyeh packed everything she needed in her sling bag. She then bid Midway a good day, thanked Brian as she handed over her plate (going straight to the kitchen herself was a bad idea—there was a ghost there very few could reckon with), and left Murklins Manor for the day.

* * *

That morning, Sadiyeh decided to pay attention to the people she passed by. It had been a little over a year since *Worlds Apart* had been rejected, after all. How had the world enjoyed her replacement book?

She would spot one of her books every now and again, on the train or through windows of cafés, mostly her older titles, which included her first ever publication, *Chickens Sleeping in My Bed*. She smirked at the memory of her fourteen-year-old self before the smile disappeared. She thought of Gordon, all warm smiles back then, so willing to take the aspiring young writer under his wing.

Work this Friday was uneventful as always, allowing her the opportunity to just sit and get lost in her thoughts.

Her shifts on Fridays were always half days. Spring had sprung, and the sun wouldn't set for another few hours, so Sadiyeh took some time to stroll around the city. She sat in the park and observed passersby, scrutinizing the books they held and hoping to catch anyone with a copy of her latest publication. No luck. She took a quick break at the local fusion restaurant and strained her ears for any conversation about her book or anyone else's, also to no avail.

Gordon was just trying to make me feel better, she thought. There was no more time to lose; Midway would likely start to worry by now, so she headed for the monorail station.

Except the usual way was blocked due to some commotion.

"Damn nudist activists!" she heard one officer yell as he rushed by, shaking his baton, with his dutiful android hot on his heels.

Sadiyeh wished the activists well for…whatever it was that they were advocating for. She decided to take an alternate route.

The Global Monorails took travelers all around the world, to every domain on the map. It could cross the Atlantic in four hours, but there were rail lines for local travel as well. Since Sadiyeh didn't own a car and didn't wish to bother Brian with transportation every day, she preferred a short trip on the monorails. It also gave her a chance to people watch, as the Midway Central Monorail Station was one of the major draws of Chicago, both for its international and local travel. Sadiyeh loved sitting and looking at people, catching glimpses of other cultures, other cities, and other worlds before a monorail came and whisked them away.

One of the greatest features of the advanced monorails, like everything electronic in the New Era, was that it ran on Tiam technology. Named after its founder at the cusp of the New Era, Tiam technology was renewable, highly efficient, and left zero carbon footprints. Because Tiam could be used on everything from the smallest devices all the way to large factories and monorails, it had rendered all previous energy resources obsolete. Sadiyeh's own laptop could operate on one-sixteenth of a Tiam battery. One monorail line, perhaps one or two Tiams.

A longer route through the city would get her to the station, but it was a bit out of her way, so she needed to hurry. She headed for the tall building nearby, took the elevator several floors up, crossed the skyway to its twin building, and headed down, passing a book concession stand.

Back outside, she wove around the bustling streets until she came upon the pedestrian overpass. It overlooked a large skatepark that from the top angle appeared like a sort of maze, easy to get lost in. At night, she hated staring down at it for too long.

As she was crossing the overpass, she heard two voices rise from below.

"*'Nay, your presence doth not whet my appetite but doth wilt it'*—yikes! What is this garbage?!" A man's laugh ricocheted off the graffitied walls down below.

Sadiyeh stopped in her tracks. Wasn't that a line from her recent book?

"Give it back!" a young woman shouted.

"I dunno why you bother reading this crap, T."

"Because she's my favorite author, ass!"

"Oh yeah? Does she always write like shit?"

Sadiyeh peered down, trying to locate the voices. She found the two surprisingly quickly, and she ran down to peek at them around the corner. The young woman, dressed to the nines in flashy jewelry, grabbed her copy of *A Thorne in Rose's Side* from her thuggish friend's hands with a grunt. Her jet-black hair was streaked with gold, and gold makeup lined her eyes, curling around her charcoal and midnight blue eyeshadow. Her attire was not something Sadiyeh could ever see herself wearing: tight jeans and a crop top, in the same hues as her eyeshadow.

In short, she was an immediate inspiration for a future character. Sadiyeh committed every detail to memory.

The young man was also fodder for inspiration, with his leather jacket, aviator sunglasses, and shoulder-length bleached blond hair that stood out against his medium-brown skin. Gold jewelry dangled around his neck and glimmered at his fingers. While his appearance seemed all around less bombastic than his partner's, there was a mysterious air about him that drew Sadiyeh in.

The woman was the first to notice Sadiyeh. "Hey, Leon." She motioned toward Sadiyeh with her chin.

Dammit! Sadiyeh wondered if she should run off, but the way the woman peered at her warmly through monolid eyes kept her glued to her place. As she sheepishly crept forward to stand in front of the two, Sadiyeh was keenly aware that several pairs of eyes were watching her from around the park. On one wall the word "NINE" was graffitied in all capital letters. Each letter was formed with images of blades of various shapes. Sadiyeh counted them quickly. Nine blades. *Nine Knives.*

"Whaddup," Leon said with a smack of his lips, earning himself a slap from the woman. "Tora! Ow!"

"Sorry for intruding," Sadiyeh said with a bow she hoped

was respectful. "I couldn't help but overhear. You didn't like the book much, did you?"

"It's good if you want something to laugh at," Leon sneered.

"God, shut up!" Tora yelled. "When was the last time you picked up a book?!"

"And when do you ever stop read—"

"It's okay," Sadiyeh interjected. "I was just debating about getting that book for a friend, and I wanted to know what others thought of it."

She glanced back around the park, studying the others silently watching her. Some rested on their skateboards, some on their hoverboards, but no one was bothering to skate at the moment. Either Leon and Tora's friends were just taking a break to watch this exchange, or this place was a hideout for a gang.

Up close, Sadiyeh noticed that Tora had tattoos reminiscent of tiger stripes across her arms and the back of her hand. Sadiyeh quickly glanced around. Every member of the group had some catlike rosettes or stripes tattooed on their hands or arms.

Nine Knives. It had a nice ring to it.

"I'd recommend a different book by the same author," Tora said. "She's normally so good! I always get a good laugh, like you can just tell she poured so much of her heart and wit into every scene! But this one...I don't know. It felt rushed. Maybe she was writing under a tight deadline. Maybe she's just been having a bad time. I guess every writer has a weakest work, and this one's it. I'd recommend something like *Tequila Tea* or *Grapes for Apes* or—oh! *Expedition of the Cowboy Cockatiels* was really good too! It depends on what your friend's into!

Mhalabiyeh writes in a few different genres, but there's stellar humor in all of them! Or I guess you can always look at her short story compilations..."

"Ah, I see," said Sadiyeh. Somehow, hearing that was both comforting and vindicating. *Take that, Gordon*, she thought. A work she had dashed off, that she barely remembered at all... she was rather glad to hear that the stupid book had been received badly, even if everyone and their dog were suddenly into flowerpeople. "Guess it really showed, then," she murmured under her breath.

"Wait a minute..." Leon's eyebrows furrowed as Tora gasped and leaned forward.

"No way!" she gasped. "You're not—or are you?!—I mean, her biography says she lives in a secluded place in a Chicago suburb—"

"How do you not know what your favorite author looks like?" Leon asked.

"Because I never had a photo in any of my books," Sadiyeh said. "But yeah, it's me. Sorry I lied about the friend part. But at least now I know this is not a book I should be handing out to all my family and friends!"

Tora's face exploded pink. "I still enjoyed it! It's just—"

"It's fine, really!" Sadiyeh laughed. "The truth is, yes, it was rushed."

She had never really had a friend before, and knowing that Tora was a dedicated reader, gangbanger or not, made her at ease enough to unload her burdens. As she told her story, more of the gang spilled around the park, lazing about like cats in the late March afternoon.

"There's another book out there?!" Tora cried, pressing her copy of *A Thorne in Rose's Side* against her lips as though praying the mysterious new book into existence right in front of her.

"Yes, but I can't publish it because it's considered too political," Sadiyeh replied, sighing. "And I can't self-publish it, either. I'm not a stranger to self-publishing, you know. I did that for my first book, before my publisher found me. But it looks like even self-publishing venues will halt production if a work mentions outer space. It's *that* controversial right now."

"Dang, I had no idea," Leon said.

"You're looking for a publisher?" Tora asked, her voice trailing.

"Yeah. I've tried everywhere, but I guess I'll either wait until this controversy settles down or keep writing useless books like this until the day I die."

Tora shifted her weight. "And you're a Magi...not that it really matters…"

Sadiyeh wasn't sure why that piece of information was relevant.

Tora glanced over at Leon, who just shrugged.

"Up to you," he said, then glanced away. "Yo, Bobbie! Get off your ass and hand me another beer!"

Sadiyeh glanced between them, but her confusion was answered when Tora reached into her back pocket and pulled out a business card.

"Here," Tora said. "We're hired by this family to help them sometimes. From what I know, they've been helping Moonchildren with all sorts of things, including publishing.

They have a publishing house—I mean, it's their business front for…what they really do."

Sadiyeh's eyes flew back to the others watching before returning to the card.

"This business is owned by Lupinites," Sadiyeh said.

"Yep." Tora nodded.

"Are you Moonchildren?"

Tora shook her head. "Just regular ole Earthchildren! We're just hired for whatever work we're ordered to do."

Earthchildren. Sadiyeh hadn't heard that term before, but whatever the case might be, if they were a gang for hire…

She turned back to the card, weighing how heavy the cardstock felt in her hand. She studied the gold-foil lettering of the logo, which was holographic when she tilted the card at an angle under the sun.

"Iridium Bay Publishing," Sadiyeh read. "Are they legitimate? I mean, won't my book just get them into trouble? This new law is even stopping self-published works! How can Lupinites fight against that?"

Tora giggled. "Wait here."

She dashed back toward the group, yelling at someone named Puma to move her tush aside, and sifted through her heavily decorated backpack before coming back with a book.

"They published this about a month after the law was passed," she said proudly, handing the book to Sadiyeh.

The cover read *Agents of Stardust* by A. R. Stellato and featured a glossy, stunning illustration of an alien surrounded by an aura of shimmering light, and a human reaching for their hand.

"It's a raunchy book, but really good," Tora said with a wink. "You can borrow it for a bit. We always hang out around here."

Still dazed by the detail of the cover, Sadiyeh thanked Tora and slipped the book and the card into her sling bag.

* * *

"Sadiyeh!" Midway said, hand over her chest by way of a greeting when Sadiyeh stepped inside. "I was getting so worried, and you didn't answer any of my calls!"

"Sorry, I missed the train," Sadiyeh said, "and I was too deep in thought to pay attention to my phone. I ended up chatting with a fan of my books."

She glanced about Murklins Manor, taking in the familiar sight of the haunted house, so cozy at this time of evening. The beige damask wallpaper bathed in soft orange candlelight, the doorknobs that looked like crystal globes. The rich, dark cherrywood archways and doors.

Music wafted from the bar in the far east wing, and if she craned her neck, she could spot a couple of patrons making their way to the hotel rooms they had reserved.

"Sadiyeh!" Brian called out from near the bar, waving a skeletal hand as he helped a recently arrived patron. "Your dinner's getting cold!"

Sadiyeh waved back at him but kept to her side of the manor, which was quite spacious for a human population of one. The living room was vast and cavernous, a common area where anyone could settle in and watch television or chat away in any of the antique, ornately carved chairs. The dining table, reserved for the tenants, was located further back.

As Sadiyeh made her way there, Franklin stepped out, rubbing his belly. He was not human, not anymore, but he was one of the few tenants Sadiyeh shared the manor with, and she greeted him warmly, even as his magnificent belch nearly blew her eardrums out.

Sadiyeh's own dinner awaited her at her favorite spot beside a large painting by one of the previous living residents, also a Magi. The painting changed to suit the beholder; for Sadiyeh, that often meant a crossword puzzle, sudoku, or a chart for her to will her creative thoughts onto and mull over as she ate.

Sadiyeh studied the card in her hand as she tucked in to her plate of sweet potatoes and rosemary chicken, the book still in her bag. A non-Moonchild gang worked for this group. There was no knowing what sort of business these Lupinites really were into. Even if Tora were friendly with them, could Sadiyeh really approach them?

"Mail, Sadiyeh," Brian announced as he set the letters beside her. She thanked him and sifted through the small pile, instantly recognizing the large envelope from her cousin Amneh Al-Ghul.

Tuning everything else out, Sadiyeh ripped the top of the envelope and pulled out her cousin's letter.

Dear Sad,
Hello Sad! How are you doing? I am doing well. I won 1st place at the scince fair, but I had to change my projict. I wanted my projict to be on the Moon. The teacher said

I had to pick somthing else. Not fair! Stupid Shela got to keep her projict!

In the end I picked dencity. Dencity is still empirtant on the Moon, right?

I hope we can vesit again soon. We keep moving house! We might be going to the Europen Domains next. I miss Murklins Manor.

Cincerely,
Amneh Bamyeh

Sadiyeh giggled at Amneh's chosen surname, recalling how the young Magi had once told Sadiyeh she wanted to grow up to become a published author just like her. And so the two had picked out a rhyming name, with *bamyeh* also being a Middle Eastern dish, this one comprised of okra in a tomato stew enjoyed over a bowl of seasoned rice.

Amneh was nine years old, and even if her letters were full of mistakes, her writing showed promise. Although Amneh had a phone by now, Sadiyeh wanted them to keep writing paper letters, both so Amneh could practice writing and so they could share the excitement of waiting for a new letter to arrive.

But...nine years old. Sadiyeh's face fell. When Amneh was younger, Sadiyeh had wanted to publish a storybook just for her, as a promise to her, but words fit for a small child never came. Too late now.

Frowning at the letter—*The teacher said I had to pick somthing else*—Sadiyeh set her fork down and made for her bedroom.

"Hello, Sadiyeh," Midway greeted.

Sadiyeh waved in reply as she sat at her writing desk. She was growing accustomed to having Midway around, both as a friend and a live-in therapist. The android would go into standby mode if Sadiyeh didn't require her assistance, which Sadiyeh appreciated. Nothing was worse than interrupted writing time.

She reread her cousin's letter before finally setting it back down. Her gaze shifted to her notebook. Scribbled on the cover were a few sketches she had made of Mercury and Pluto from *Worlds Apart*, along with some characters from *Uranus in Virgo*.

Not fair! Amneh's words echoed in her mind once more.

Sadiyeh took out the business card from Tora, staring at the logo and phone number.

"So, we're really doing this," she mumbled under her breath.

Phone in hand, she drew a deep breath, steadied her heart, and dialed the number.

* * *

Downtown Chicago • March 25, 893 NE

When Sadiyeh first reached the hotel she had been instructed to go to, she almost wondered if she had gotten lost. The building, tall enough to scrape the sky, looked far too grandiose to function as a publishing office. Right past the front entrance lay a spacious lobby, the marble floor echoing her every footstep. A reception desk stood to her left, and adjacent to it was a café, divided from the hotel by a wall of pure crystal glass pane. Far on the other side was a row of golden-rimmed elevators. She spotted the large double doors to the hotel's famous theater, along with a few of the many conference suites this place was also known for. Unsurprisingly, there were a few androids alongside the human workers.

A directory nearby confirmed her suspicions that the entire building was over fifty stories, renovated during the early years of the New Era. The floors above her comprised conference halls and hotel suites, but there was also an arcade, a gym, swimming pool, and a cinema.

The thought of how much it would cost to stay here for one night made her queasy.

Everywhere around her were gold decorations that must have come straight from the Old Era, restored such that they shone brighter than ever before. The entire ground floor was a mishmash of the antique and the modern, an embrace of old Chicago and a celebration of its survival into the New Era.

Sadiyeh debated asking the heavily perfumed receptionist at the front desk if she was in the right place but decided against it. She didn't exactly want anyone to know she was about to conduct business with the Lupinite mafia.

Suddenly one of golden elevators dinged, and out stepped a tall man flanked by a handful other Lupinites, all sharply dressed.

That could only be Tetsu Gushiken, Lupinite and founder of Iridium Bay Publishing. With his slicked-back hair that was greying at the temples and the crow's feet around his eyes, he looked about twenty years older than her. Every now and then, he cracked a wicked grin at something one of the other Lupinites said. A pack of cigarettes was tucked neatly into the breast pocket of his expensive, impeccably tailored suit. His dark eyes shone with an intense inner light, the wolf spirit burning just below the surface.

Every step he took across the marble lobby demanded respect, attention, cooperation, fear. Even his simplest gesture enchanted all those around him. The others looked at him with deep admiration. Sadiyeh stopped in her tracks, her breath stolen, unsure if she wanted to run away or stay rooted in place. She couldn't tear her eyes from him.

The tall, ropy man closest to Gushiken caught her staring and glared at her threateningly, his canines bared.

Sadiyeh yelped.

Gushiken turned to look at her, his full lips quirking into a small grin.

"Sadiyeh Mhalabiyeh?" he asked.

She nodded, glancing nervously at each of the other Lupinites.

"Y-yes, sir!" she said and bowed respectfully.

Was that a snicker she just heard from one of his men? Were they converging around her, ready to pounce? Would the receptionist at the front desk do anything if they took her away?

She trembled under their scrutiny, jumping when she felt the weight of Gushiken's large hand on her shoulder.

"Pleasure to meet you! Follow me."

He led her on a small tour through the ground floor and introduced her to everyone: the heavily perfumed receptionist, the chefs crafting artisanal sandwiches in the ground floor café, even the janitors.

"You own the Blackstone Hotel?" Sadiyeh asked breathlessly.

A hundred or even fifty years ago, the thought of a Lupinite having this much money was simply unheard of.

Gushiken smiled at her question. "That I do. I only take the best for my family."

She couldn't imagine that the acquisition of this antique property had been peaceful. Money alone wasn't enough if the interested party was Lupinite. But they were powerful, she could see *that* clearly. *Treat them like monsters and they will start acting like monsters*, she thought.

Sadiyeh memorized as many names and faces as she could, quickly realizing that nearly everyone she met was either an android or a Moonchild. Other Magi, Lupinites, Desmonites. She searched for any signs of discomfort in their smiles, any signs that they feared working under Gushiken, but she found none.

Somewhat comforted, she followed Gushiken up the elevator to the publishing house. The upper stories gave a clear view of the lake and the antique Buckingham Fountain.

Iridium Bay Publishing took up an entire floor, with only a small stretch of open hallway leading from the elevator to a closed door on the other side, presumably Gushiken's office. The stretch of wall was made of hardwood, forged in an intricate design. A large pane of glass divided this stretch from the rest of the publishing house, so that everyone working in the office could get a good view of who was coming in and going out.

The office was swathed in warm sunlight, thanks to the countless number of windows lining the floor. People worked in cubicles, but Sadiyeh could hear friendly chatter, keyboards clicking away, laughter. Everyone seemed relaxed here.

Wordlessly, Gushiken made for the door across from the elevator. Two of his companions stayed with him. One was the tall man who had glared at her earlier. The other was a stocky woman with short hair, a perpetual frown, and a pockmarked face full of scars.

Sadiyeh, unsure where else to go, followed Gushiken.

"Raine, be a dear and get the door," Gushiken ordered once they were inside his office.

The stocky Lupinite woman bowed her head, giving Sadiyeh an odd look as she passed by her to close the door before standing guard in front of a steel safe. Sadiyeh's heart leapt to her throat.

Gushiken walked around to his executive desk, made of a deep, polished mahogany, and motioned for her to take a seat. She sank into a large chair and, under the scrutiny of three pairs of sharp eyes, instantly felt smaller and more vulnerable. The only thing that somewhat calmed her was seeing that Gushiken had a printed copy of her manuscript on his desk.

Gushiken motioned toward the tall man as he pulled a cigarette from his pack. Sadiyeh watched as the man lit Gushiken's cigarette in practiced, smooth movements before being rewarded with a kiss to the inside of his palm. That earned Gushiken a caress on the cheek that quickly turned into a slap. Sadiyeh nearly jumped out of her seat, but Gushiken chuckled, watching the man retreat with an expression that mirrored the same adoration the other Lupinites had previously shown him.

"Welcome, Sadiyeh," Gushiken said, finally addressing her. The cigarette hung between his fingers gracefully as he leaned back in his leather chair. "I'm afraid not even the smoke can mask your smell."

"Pardon?" Sadiyeh squeaked.

"We can smell fear on you. Be assured, our Mooncousin, there is nothing to be afraid of while you are here."

Oh, damn! Sadiyeh bowed. The tall Lupinite man narrowed his eyes. It didn't help her nerves, but Gushiken didn't seem put off.

"I'm sorry!" Sadiyeh said hurriedly. "I'm just nervous, that's all!"

Gushiken waved his hand, instantly silencing her.

"First, introductions. You will come to know all my family eventually. With us right now is my second captain, Raine Garrett. You might have seen her patrolling the city with her crew."

"Nice to meet you, sweetcakes," Garrett said, flashing her canines.

"My second-in-command and first captain is Connor Bailey, also known as my obnoxious husband."

"Oh, fuck off!" Bailey spat at Gushiken, and Sadiyeh startled once more.

To Sadiyeh, Bailey gave a solemn nod. "Pleasure," he said in a tone completely different from how he had addressed his husband just a moment ago.

So he was the underboss. Oh, great.

Bailey, too, was on the handsome side. He had long dark wavy hair that reached his shoulders, and a little bit of a beard. Steel-grey eyes studied Sadiyeh carefully. Did he notice how Sadiyeh had been studying Gushiken? Was he being territorial?

As a writer, she wanted to convey to Bailey, *Gushiken would make an interesting character! He*—

Her mind filled her with an image of being pressed against the wall by Gushiken, blade against her throat, canine fangs piercing her shoulders as he—

She coughed and readjusted herself on her seat.

"Nice to meet all of you," Sadiyeh said timidly, bowing to each of them.

"It is an honor having you over today, Child of Sahariel," Gushiken said.

Sadiyeh blushed. Moonchildren almost never addressed one another by mentioning the clan's respective Moon Daughter.

"Thank you for agreeing to see me on such a short notice, um, Child of Dhibiniel," Sadiyeh said, and after a few awkward silent moments, added, "It's not often I venture to this part of Chicago. I mean, I work in the city. My old publisher also had an office here. But it's such a big city! I never stopped to really explore."

Bailey paced behind her as if slowly circling his prey. Garrett remained in place, as still as an android. Sadiyeh's eyes bolted around the room, noting a display of swords behind the executive desk. She didn't want to speculate on what could be in the safe. The office was just the right size to hold a couple more people, but small enough to corner a victim.

"Oh?" Gushiken said with a smile. "Where do you live?"

Sadiyeh hesitated. She was about to entrust him with her book, her heart and soul, but giving away the location of Murklins Manor would be a grave breach of trust to Brian. And she wasn't exactly sure if someone like him should know…

"South side," she said.

"Da suburbs," Bailey said casually. "Da slummy, humble

suburbs." His face broke into a fond smile. "I grew up der. Good times."

"Plenty of forests to run around naked in," Gushiken said.

"I never did dat."

Gushiken cocked his eyebrow at Sadiyeh.

"Fine, *once*!"

"The time when I found you bleeding to death. You were trying to fight off an entire mob all by yourself."

"For fuck's sake, so I was! I survived, didn' I?!"

Sadiyeh turned to Garrett, who rolled her eyes. She stepped forward and whispered in Sadiyeh's ear, "The boss loves to rile Bailey up. Let them be."

Satisfied with having messed around with his husband a little more, Gushiken turned back to Sadiyeh. "Just give us the word. We'd love to have you over at our headquarters on the north side."

North side? Sadiyeh's eyes widened. The part of Chicago where houses ran for millions of international dollars. Just how much money did they have?

"Thank you," she said feebly.

The mad glint in Bailey's eyes disappeared as fast as it had sparked. He resumed pacing slowly behind Sadiyeh as Gushiken skimmed through her manuscript.

"We received a call from Tora about you shortly before getting the pleasure of hearing from you ourselves. You do have an impressive résumé, Sadiyeh."

"Thank you, sir," Sadiyeh said. She hesitated before asking, "Um, have you…read my books before?"

"Only a couple, I'm afraid," Gushiken said. "I was a far

more voracious reader in my youth. But I must say you do have an incredible way of gripping your readers."

"Th-thank you."

"And this is only one book?"

"Y-yes. I have another book. It's mostly done. I was thinking of calling it *Uranus in Virgo*."

Bailey gave a curt, maniacal guffaw behind her. One side of Gushiken's face twitched in amusement.

"Mhalabiyeh…I recognize da name," Bailey spoke up. "I've read yer stuff before."

"Oh! You have?" Sadiyeh spun around, eager to keep things civil with the odd Lupinite.

"Ya look surprised dat I know how to read!" he said, his voice cold and accusatory as he paused to stare down at her. Sadiyeh yelped. Garrett sighed audibly. Bailey recovered and resumed his pacing. "Tora recommended yer works to me, said it'd cheer my sister up when she went for her dialysis. Gotta say, yer shit's done its magic."

"Thank you," Sadiyeh said. "I'm sorry to hear about your sister."

"Don' say it like she's already dead!" Bailey snapped. "Finley's a fighter like da rest of da family!"

Sadiyeh didn't ask him to elaborate on his definition of family.

"I hope she recovers all the same," Sadiyeh said. "I went to the hospital last year. It wasn't pleasant."

"I'm 'fraid her situation's permanent," Bailey said. "We've looked into having a transplant, but no luck findin' a matchin' donor. Pity we can' just get a cybernetic kidney."

Sadiyeh bowed her head solemnly. "Reyrson's law of biomechatronics, passed in 298 NE. Beyond limbs or eyes, a human may not undergo further cybernetic modifications to their body."

"You sure know your history," Gushiken commented.

"I read a lot," Sadiyeh said. "Um, my books, the Hikmat duology, are centered around the main criticisms that arose due to Reyrson's law. You might not wish to get those for Finley—I mean, there are characters who die because they don't have access to cybernetic organs because of Reyrson's law."

Bailey bowed his head graciously. "Appreciate it, ma'am."

Gushiken, who had been watching their little exchange with a smile, turned her manuscript back to the first page.

Meanwhile, Garrett, as if on cue, took a step forward. "I did my homework on you after you called the office. You say you don't venture much into the world, yet you seem to know a lot about it."

Sadiyeh blushed. "Like I said, I read a lot. I do talk with people who...visit my place of residence. I'm not *that* sheltered! I just like my peace and quiet, so I can focus on writing."

"You certainly do seem prolific. Helps not to have distractions."

"Yeah, well...my first publication was when I was fourteen. I self-published my book."

"A young entrepreneur! I like that!" Gushiken's suave smile ran through her spine.

"I-I only did it to see if I could. And it sold really well! That was when my current company found me and then republished it a few years later. But I didn't publish anything new for years after that…I had school, and I was nervous about what to publish next. I kept writing but didn't settle on a project for a while."

"But when you did, you wrote *Federal Reserve Goat*," Garrett said. "Considering the mess that transpired five years ago, your book was rather prophetic."

"Is that part of your magic?" Gushiken asked.

Sadiyeh shook her head. "I don't believe so. I just read a lot and think a lot. I'm always lost in my thoughts."

And sometimes I write based on my dreams, but that story is still incomplete.

"Deep thinkers usually make the best seers," Gushiken said with a wave of his hand. "I'm interested in why you are now looking to publish with us. It appears your last publication with OakFinch Press wasn't that long ago."

"Yeah, well…see, I wrote *that* book in place of the manuscript you currently have," Sadiyeh said and then went over her tale. Gushiken's sly smile deepened the longer she spoke, and she wondered if she was walking right into the monster's jaws.

"We will take it."

"What?"

"We will gladly accept your book, cousin."

Sadiyeh stared at Gushiken, taken aback. "Wait, really? Just like that?!"

Gushiken nodded.

She was keenly aware of Bailey circling her like a shark ready to sink his jaws in at any moment.

"You are a Moonchild seeking aid," Gushiken explained.

"We offer aid to Moonchildren, a voice for those silenced in recent times. It's as simple as that."

"Without any stipulations?"

A grin broke across his devilishly handsome face. "Whatever could you mean?"

Garrett raised her eyebrows in mild amusement.

"Say it," Bailey hissed.

Sadiyeh sighed. What had she gotten herself into? "You are a Rioter. Your business is a front for your criminal activities."

"That it is, but it doesn't stop the fact that we *do* have a publishing house, we *do* own a hotel, and we *do* own every other business in this building, and many other businesses in the city. Most of our employees are fellow Moonchildren, and they are paid well."

"How are your book sales?"

"Iridium Bay Publishing has been in business for about twenty years. Our books have sold well enough to keep our authors afloat. You will be given 75 percent of the royalties."

"Seriously? That's an insane amount compared to any publisher!"

Gushiken chuckled darkly. "We have little need of the money ourselves, dear Sadiyeh."

"Then how do you afford printing? The electricity bills for the office?"

"All of our funding comes from money we receive from off-record business deals. We only ask for payment from the non-Moonchildren we deal with."

"Ah…in other words…protection money and extortion." If their headquarters were up north, then they must have been swimming in pure gold. Money they'd gotten from all the usual ways mobs made their living.

As a little girl, Sadiyeh had heard about the Lupinite mafias, known as Riots, from some of the regulars visiting Murklins Manor. As the United Domains had slowly backed out of sending aid to them over the last several decades, some rose to fight back, taking matters into their own hands. What began as Lupinite families watching out for one another and fellow Moonchildren in their communities soon turned into criminal syndicates composed of large families, bound by blood, loyalty, or often both, all striving for the same goal.

Their influence had grown steadily over the years, but never did Sadiyeh think she would be here, requiring their aid herself. She stared at her manuscript. Gordon had failed her. The United Domains had failed her. But could she trust someone who made her cower in her seat?

"Only from the non-Moonchildren do we require money," Gushiken reiterated. "It is our Mooncousins that we protect to the death, for we are the most vulnerable. I have a brother and sister in the East Asian Domain and the West European Domain respectively who are bringing with them this new philosophy. We hope to spread this new era through the entire world. If the United Domains will neglect us, then we will be the protectors we have been destined to be from the beginning—as the ancient stories tell."

Great, so they've appointed themselves as the Robin Hoods of the New Era. They were also her only shot at getting this book out there.

Something snapped inside Sadiyeh, and she couldn't help

but meet Gushiken's eyes. "So you're crooked, but I suppose that doesn't make you worse than the United Domains themselves."

"What was dat?" Bailey cried out.

Gushiken raised a hand.

"You seem bitter toward the United Domains," Gushiken observed.

"Of course I'm bitter," Sadiyeh replied. "I love my history, as you can see. I hold on to whatever we still have that hasn't been lost to the Black Sun. I had been hoping we could learn more, shed more light on the Moonchildren especially, but then...one tiny discovery and suddenly we're closing shop on all discussions around space travels and the Moon? Look at how it's turned our lives upside down in less than a year! People don't want stories about stupid flowerpeople! People still have questions they'll now never get the answers to! It may be small now, but I fear it may lead to a third—a third..."

Gushiken quirked an eyebrow. "A third intifada?"

Sadiyeh nodded. "The first two were peaceful. But who's to say the third wouldn't be a bloodbath?"

His chuckle came like a smooth growl. "All because they're blocking creatives from expressing themselves?"

Now he was goading *her*!

"They're stopping science! They've completely shut the door to an entire field! It's probably more impactful on society than what artists do, but even still, why the obsession with silencing even artists? How can art hurt anyone?!"

Gushiken and Bailey shared an amused look, a secret glance, as though the two had previously discussed the matter between themselves.

"I would not be as uncharitable," Gushiken said. "For one, this move by the United Domains has greatly helped our business over the past year."

Sadiyeh glared at him. Of course the law would please him! How long had A. R. Stellato been publishing with them? With her nerves she couldn't recall the number of years, but she knew Stellato was a longtime client.

"The new law doesn't impact you at all?" she asked.

"We have our own ways of dealing with it."

"I knew you were going to say that."

"You do not seem pleased, Sadiyeh."

Sadiyeh swallowed thickly. "It's just…I'm so used to my old publisher!"

"Change is always terrifying, isn't it?"

Sadiyeh let out a small snort. "Everything would have been fine had that stupid law never existed, had that stupid discovery not been made!"

"Had the government never been erected," Gushiken added.

Sadiyeh paused. Would she go that far? Tentatively, she peered up at Gushiken, wondering if he was merely toying with her. She couldn't read his expression. Should she agree, being in the presence of a werewolf mob?

"I…I guess so," Sadiyeh began slowly. "Looking through history, I think we've seen more harm from them than good. Prior to the year 425 NE, we were content to live and function as small tribes. We saw no need for country borders, with so much having been lost to the Floods."

"Did we?" Gushiken challenged. "Had the United Domains

never been formed, we would not have been able to prevent the epidemic from spreading out of the northeastern tip from the Northeast American Domain and infecting the whole world."

"They achieved that by bombing the entire region!" Sadiyeh said hotly. "And we did not wish to see borders!"

"The First Intifada concluded with a truce," Gushiken reminded her. "We got some say on how the thirteen domains could be divided up."

"I suppose…and we did win the Second Intifada," Sadiyeh said.

"Did we really?" Gushiken said. "We fought against a draconian law dictating how many children each household can have, forcing parenthood on some and gender assignment and respective roles on others. All in the name of keeping order and the human population from going out of control when we have so little land left, with everything lost to floods and radiation? We may have won, and the human population has increased in the last three hundred years and will undoubtedly continue to expand. You do not think they will find other ways to suppress us? Perhaps they have already begun."

"Oh, Moon Mother!" Sadiyeh gasped as the cold dread crept back into her. She wished Midway were next to her. "I see the big picture now! They…they really *are* trying to erase us, aren't they?" Why did she even think of ever holding a morsel of respect for the United Domains?

"You're scaring her," Garrett pointed out coolly. Her nostrils flared. "It's not all bad, sweetcakes. Without the United Domains, we wouldn't have had the worldwide effort in setting up the Global Monorails."

Sadiyeh, staring at her feet, gave a little nod.

"Nor da organization and resources to steamroll android production," Bailey added. "Woulda been a shame leaving Myla's legacy in da dust, ya think?"

"They stood by the side of the people and defended the use of Tiam technology when a vocal minority tried to push for reverting to the old and destructive methods of consuming fossil fuels," Gushiken said.

Sadiyeh sighed heavily. "You're all right! We need the United Domains. They do protect us; they are helping us proceed through the New Era! But they've also hurt us! They've been chipping away at our rights! They're targeting *us*!"

"Which is why people such as my family exist," Gushiken said. "Like it or not, the Riots and the government are two sides of the same coin—both necessary evils you must embrace in your life.

"So what will it be then, Sadiyeh?"

Sadiyeh stared at her manuscript. What other option did she have? Even now, she still wished she could convince Gordon to take her two titles, and she had tried, repeatedly, but he had been firm: OakFinch Press would no longer publish any books involving space or the Moon.

"Show me the contract," she said.

After Bailey placed the form in front of her, she took her time dissecting every line. She wished she could conjure up Muse and have them help her pick apart the contract, but she didn't out of fear of the Rioters harming Muse in any way.

"Sign when you are ready, love," Gushiken said, his voice near her ear.

A shiver ran up Sadiyeh's spine. She took her prized pen out of her pocket and held it over the contract.

This is it, she thought. This was the defining moment of her life. Either she would come to regret this decision, or it would prove to be a turning point for the better. She just had to trust Tetsu Gushiken, Moonchild to Moonchild.

With her heart racing, Sadiyeh signed her name on the dotted line.

Chapter 3

Muddy Middles

Spring 893 NE

The Vine siblings had been tasked with preparing Sadiyeh's book. Two Magis who lived in the heart of Chicago, they often stayed overnight at their offices at the Blackstone Hotel. Their cubicles faced away from each other, but that didn't stop them from engaging in small talk throughout the day.

The entire atmosphere of Iridium Bay Publishing was one of serenity, tranquility, and safety. The fact that the Vine siblings worked so near the Rioters didn't faze them one bit. Or perhaps they had already grown accustomed to these affairs by the time Sadiyeh joined them.

The former seemed more likely, as everyone involved with Iridium Bay Publishing saw the office as a kind of sanctuary. Even clients were welcome to stay however long they wished. Sadiyeh suspected that Gushiken didn't mind if one or two stayed overnight if they didn't want to sleep in any of the hotel suites. The Blackstone Hotel had its nighttime guards as well, either Moonchildren or androids. Their clients were safe.

A small communal kitchen had been set up, and the fridge

was always stuffed with food. As an occasional treat, Gushiken or one of his men would order catering from the hotel's kitchens for everyone.

Couches lined the walls of the office, making it an ideal place to sit back and read, socialize, or simply get away. More and more often in the coming years, Sadiyeh would find herself stopping by the building as she grew more comfortable in the presence of the Lupinites.

And because of Maria Vine.

Gushiken had personally taken Sadiyeh to meet the Vine siblings. Russell Vine, a heavyset black man with an infectious laugh, set to sketching out the cover for *Worlds Apart*. He conversed with her for a time about her book, having devoured the manuscript after getting hooked by the first line alone. The walls of his station displayed his artwork from previous projects, and Sadiyeh's heart leapt when she recognized the cover of *Agents of Stardust* among them.

Her cover was going to look as amazing as that book's.

Russell's younger sister, Maria, was also rather giddy and prone to giggles, which made her black eyes glimmer with magic and mirth. Her long hair, styled in mini twists that reached her hips, would bounce around her heart-shaped face every time the fits of laughter struck. Her face, ethereally beautiful with a smooth complexion, could shift quickly from playful to a deep scowl as she pored through Sadiyeh's manuscript, picking her words apart. As easily amused as Maria was, Sadiyeh had learned that she possessed a sharp eye for detail.

When Gushiken had introduced her to Maria, Sadiyeh

could barely string two words together. She blushed the whole time Maria spoke.

Am I just going to fall in love with everyone I meet here? Sadiyeh wondered, catching herself as she studied Maria hard at work, mumbling now and again, giving a tiny cry of victory after killing a typo or gushing over a turn of phrase that she particularly liked.

Neither Maria nor Russell incorporated magic in their profession the way Sadiyeh had gotten Muse to help her with writing. Instead, they used magic in simple tasks such as stirring sugar in their tea or growing tiny pots of herbs that lined the windows of their office space. Simple, everyday magic that any Magi could perform.

Odd, Sadiyeh thought, but she didn't ask them about it.

Within two weeks, both siblings had revision notes and a cover ready for Sadiyeh to review. The following month, *Worlds Apart* was finally released into the world, with work already underway on *Uranus in Virgo*.

"I'm so happy for you!" Tora said as Sadiyeh passed by the gang one evening. "The book's fantastic! Absolutely brilliant!"

"She's been in stitches all day," Leon said grumpily. "Practically begging us all to read it—*read*! Can you imagine that?"

"Trust me, you won't suddenly turn into literary snobs with my sort of books," Sadiyeh said. "Try it with some beer! Make a drinking game out of it!"

"She's really funny!" Tora said, grabbing hold of Leon's arm.

Sadiyeh, about to leave them, stopped and turned back around. "Hey, Leon. How do you know an omen is promiscuous? It comes in threes."

Tora shrieked with laughter. Leon stared, open-mouthed. "Wait, wha—what the!"

Sadiyeh grinned. "A little sample of my naughtier humor. You'll find more in *Worlds Apart*."

"Hey, Tora, babe, let me read that."

At the monorail station, Sadiyeh spotted a few others with her book and heard a stifled snigger here and there.

Laughter. Joy. All because of her. A bittersweet smile spread across her face.

Finally. Everyone was finally reading the book she had held onto for so long.

The story that had come to her while she lay dying.

* * *

Back at home, Brian interrupted Sadiyeh halfway through dinner.

"Apologies, but a Mr. Gordon is on the line, requesting to speak with you," he said.

Sadiyeh ran to the hotel reception area and picked up the old-fashioned receiver. From her vantage point she had a clear view of the bar patrons. Two ghosts were currently at it with an animated story while a zombie sat between them, his sole remaining eye glazed over and a shot glass of formaldehyde in front of him.

"Gordon?"

"Sadiyeh! I just heard about your newest book. I wish to extend my congratulations. But…" Although there was no hint of anger in his voice, she couldn't help but flinch. "I have to admit, I am startled."

"Why? It's the same book I presented to you last year."

"And you know why we couldn't take it."

"This company did."

"And they're dealing with the regulations okay?"

"They're handling things just fine. I'm neither the first nor the last to publish about space after the law passed. My next book's also about space."

Silence followed. Sadiyeh could just imagine sweat wetting the collar around Gordon's thick, ruddy neck.

"Sadiyeh…I'm afraid your new book may cause trouble for our company."

She stared as one of the ghosts whacked the other; the zombie's shoulders quivered as he silently laughed.

"Why? You weren't the one to print it!"

"No, but we do print your other books."

"And…what I just did might tarnish OakFinch's pristine reputation?"

"Something like that."

"So…you're saying you might drop me?"

"Afraid so. We may be required to stop printing all your books. It is nothing personal, Sadiyeh, but we have the company's image to uphold."

Guess I'll just sign off everything to Gushiken, Sadiyeh thought. *He is going to have a hexin' field day!*

"Well, if that's what you have to do, then I can't stop you," Sadiyeh said, trying to keep her voice steady. "It was a pleasure working with you, Mr. Gordon, and with OakFinch Press. I regret that it had to come to this."

She hung up. Her appetite ruined, Sadiyeh bid Brian good night and returned to her room.

"Sadiyeh?" Midway asked, her eyes lighting up, obviously having registered Sadiyeh's soured mood. Sadiyeh ushered her away with a wave of her hand.

"I just need to be alone for a moment," Sadiyeh said. "I'm not ready to talk."

Once Midway was out of the room, Sadiyeh collapsed on her canopy bed and stared at the ceiling, letting the tears fall. With her prized pen, she drew little fluorescent flowers, butterflies, and swallows midair, the sort of flora and fauna she imagined could exist on some alien planet. She watched, arms folded under her head, as they glowed above her.

"I don't care about ever getting married," she said aloud softly to herself. "I don't care about ever doing anything more than my current lab job. I'm okay with living the rest of my days in Murklins Manor. I just want to write, to keep creating new stories, new worlds. I just want to create. I never meant to cause trouble for anyone. I never meant for my existence to be a nuisance for anyone. I just want a space I can exist in freely.

"Why is that asking for too much?"

* * *

Gushiken was more than pleased to take on the books OakFinch Press had dropped. He immediately called up Russell Vine to illustrate new covers for all the new editions—thirteen books in total.

"You owe me lunch *and* dinner for the rest of the year and the next!" Russell chided Gushiken in a tone Sadiyeh would never have dared to use on a mob boss.

But Gushiken simply laughed. "I'll even take you out to the movies."

The covers came steadily throughout the summer, and Gushiken paid Russell quite well for his illustrations. And while Sadiyeh loved having a matching set in her bedroom library, she lamented the end of a many-years-long relationship with her former publisher.

With *Uranus in Virgo* out of the way, she turned back to the draft she'd had on the back burner prior to...well, the incident on New Year's Eve.

"Ah, the Bandit Budgies," she said under her breath. Stars of a sequel to *Expedition of the Cowboy Cockatiels*. What sort of mischief would these birds get up to?

Thinking of her morally ambiguous new friends, she settled on a heist. *Heist of the Bandit Budgies* it was.

* * *

Every so often Sadiyeh would run into fellow clients of the company: Moonchildren who sought a place to stay awhile, or other creatives who stopped by and made the office their second home. There was one Desmonite who, from what Sadiyeh understood, published photography books. She happened by them one evening submitting their manuscript and a set of photo originals. They winked at Sadiyeh, then went to a window and opened the latch. They exposed their back, revealing a tattoo of bat wings, which then transformed into actual wings, and right before Sadiyeh's eyes, the Desmonite turned into a bat and flew off into the night.

"Didn't even stop for a drink?" Gushiken said with a shake of his head, walking by as he casually wiped blood off his hands with a towel. Sadiyeh flinched but pretended she hadn't seen anything.

Like the Vine siblings, she had learned to turn a blind eye every time the Lupinite family's other business leaked into their office. True to his word, neither Gushiken nor any of his family members had ever laid a finger on Sadiyeh or any of the Moonchildren, and never once had she felt that her safety was compromised.

That didn't make these little brushes with violence any easier to swallow, though. Passing by a Lupinite armed with a gun and wondering if any bullets had been fired, or spotting bloodstains on a blade…the suggestion of violence was just as distressing as being directly involved. A couple of times she didn't see the Nine Knives when she left work, and she hoped they were eating out at a pizzeria or playing at an arcade instead of running a mission for the Riot. The thought of any of them not surviving into the next day kept her up at night.

"How did you all meet?" Sadiyeh asked Tora one summer night as they sat on the steps of the skater park. Her biggest fan hugged a signed copy *Uranus in Virgo* close to her chest as though it were a stuffed toy she'd won at a fair.

"Me and Gushiken, or the gang?" Tora asked.

"Both, I guess."

"Gushiken and his men saved us from some unsavory folks years back," Tora explained. "We owe them our lives. As for the gang, I found every single one of my sibs. Some had been orphaned. Some had been kicked out of their homes. I sniffed each of them out. Gave them a place to stay. Gave them food. Gave them work, mainly through Gushiken. Not the most honest of work, but we get by. We're all that we have."

Tora smiled as the two of them watched the gang passing by on their skateboards and hoverboards. They shouted and hollered at one another. One of them, Agu, challenged Leon to see who could fly higher on the launch ramp.

"But you're all so young," Sadiyeh mused. "The United Domains did nothing to help you while you were homeless?"

Tora snorted. "The homeless are invisible in their eyes. The United Domains don't care about a lot of people. I mean, you know about that already."

Cheers followed nearby; Agu won, having flown just one inch higher than Leon.

"Thank you, by the way, for introducing me to Gushiken," Sadiyeh said. "Sometimes I'm not sure if it was the best decision—"

"Ah, why?" Tora giggled.

Blushing, Sadiyeh told Tora all about what had happened with Gordon.

"That's horrible your old publisher just shut you out!" Tora said. "And here I thought we were just getting a new edition of everything! Well, at least Iridium Bay is more stable than relying on someone held at the mercy of the United Domains!"

"Yeah," Sadiyeh said. "I still wonder what the United Domains are really trying to do. They claim it's new scientific information, but then why go through such lengths to silence even a fantasy book just because it has a space theme? They're not coming out and outright saying it's an attack on Moonchildren, but it sure feels like it."

"I bet they're hiding aliens," Tora said.

Sadiyeh snorted loudly.

"What? Don't think I'm right?"

Sadiyeh wasn't certain how to answer that. The Moonchildren had been hoping they would get answers about themselves, where they came from, why the Moon was so important to them... "I mean..."

"Think about it!" Tora set her book on her lap and threw out her arms, waving them toward the sky. "Big, wide universe! Innumerable stars and planets and galaxies spanning the cosmos! And yet life only exists on planet Earth?" Her tone changed at the end to one of incredulity and bitterness, accompanied with a roll of her eyes.

Sadiyeh laughed. "Makes sense. So why would the United Domains cover all that up?"

"Who knows?" Tora said, rubbing her chin. "Maybe they're worried they might have competition for political power."

"An alien overlord ruling the United Domains? Okay, now that you bring that up..."

"I would like an alien leader!"

"Me too!"

Sadiyeh grinned up at Tora, taking note of her necklaces. One in particular caught her attention: a spiral. A Fibonacci spiral.

The golden ratio. Sacred geometry. Sadiyeh couldn't explain why, but the idea instantly stuck with her.

Ride the spiral, she thought as she studied the night sky. She filed the words into the back of her mind.

* * *

Sadiyeh wasn't sure if she simply hadn't noticed them before, but after signing on with Iridium Bay Publishing, she began to see more of Gushiken's men around the city, watching her as she went to and from work. It unnerved her at first, spotting them from the corner of her eye as they stood by a pillar or behind a vending machine, usually keeping their distance. They weren't that hard to miss. Look for a sharply dressed person with strikingly wolfish good looks, and they were likely to be a member of the family, a Rioter.

They ensured she got to work on time, sometimes pulling her away from traffic and escorting her right to her train. They saw to it she got home safely. Once or twice, they drove her home, as far as she would allow them before she got out and walked the rest of the way. She had been surprised how well they complied with her wishes. Her business was hers. They never asked questions.

She encountered the Nine Knives more often outside their little hideout, spotting them by their catlike rosettes or the striped tattoos on their cheeks, arms, and hands. Brief and sudden were their encounters, be it a member giving her a wink from across the street or another skating by slowly and bowing with a proper "Good evening, ma'am."

* * *

The tug came out of nowhere as Sadiyeh was about to cross the street.

"Wha-*hey*!"

"Not that way, sweetcakes."

Sadiyeh spun around. It was Raine Garrett. The woman led her in the opposite direction. Nothing in her expression informed Sadiyeh as to why they were going that way. Sadiyeh glanced back but couldn't see any danger or heavy traffic in the area.

"Um, what's happening?"

"Here." Garrett ushered Sadiyeh into a taxi at the next block, facing the lake. Sadiyeh plopped onto the back seat and was joined by Garrett.

"Where to, Captain?" the driver asked.

Another Lupinite. Sadiyeh stared. Did the Rioters also own a taxi company? Just how much control did they exert over the city?

"Take the scenic route, Petrov," Garrett said. "This one's gonna get ugly."

"What's going on?" Sadiyeh asked.

"Oh, the nudist activists will be at it again soon," Garrett said with a tiny, mischievous grin. "Soon pigs will be swarming the place."

Sadiyeh stared at Garrett and then at Petrov before it dawned on her. "Wait…do you have something to do with these activists?"

Garrett's grin widened, exposing her canines. "What gives you that idea, sweetcakes?"

Sadiyeh laughed. Should she even be surprised at this point? "*What* are they even protesting?"

"Haven't been keeping with the news?"

"No…"

"That's all right, hon. We're just protesting the unlawful incarceration of Antonio Spritz."

"You?"

"Oh, yes. He's one politician at the United Domains you *want* to keep. Quite friendly with Lupinites. Worked his flat ass off to ensure our kind got better treatment in the workplace so more of us don't end up down the path of the Riots."

Sadiyeh furrowed her brow. She hadn't stopped to think how the Rioters viewed themselves. Of course, not every Lupinite was one. Rioters would rather that less of their kind ended up needing to resort to this sort of life…

Garrett went on. "Some didn't like the fact that our family and Spritz had swapped money under the table. The way we see it, the pigs were just looking for a reason to lock him up."

"Ah."

Petrov drove them around the corner, and sure enough, Sadiyeh heard sirens and shouts from police officers. Chants of "Tits for Spritz! Coppers are the pits!" filled the vicinity before the taxi turned a corner and drove them away from the pandemonium.

Grateful she hadn't gotten caught up in the mess, Sadiyeh made a mental note to get Garrett and her chauffeur a gift.

It soon became a habit for her to stash tiny breakfast treats in her sling bag to hand to any Rioter or Nine Knives member she happened by on her way to work, as neither were difficult to notice. She even knew some by name, what they liked and disliked, and whether they had any dietary restrictions.

Seeing the surprise followed by gratitude reflected in that wolfish glint in their eyes made it all worth it for her. She had to remind herself that the Lupinites had been among the first impacted by the United Domains. They were Rioters because they had no other option in life. They were used to having so little. They had built an empire for themselves out of scraps, fighting to live under crushing constraints.

She no longer felt afraid walking alone at night on the streets of Chicago. The long winter nights drew her out more, and she enjoyed the outdoor winter holiday decorations, taking in the gentle jazz music that wafted through the air of her beloved city.

At home she found herself missing them, her friends and protectors. Sometimes she would climb up to the roof of Murklins Manor at night to write and to glance out to the northeast, pretending she could make out the skyline of Chicago, pretending she lived there instead of in the humble suburbs, tucked away from society in the middle of a forest. As her pen slid through the pages of her notebook, her thoughts drifted back to the Blackstone Hotel, to the Lupinite Riot, to Gushiken…

She heard howling of wolves one night as she slept. Had they found out where she lived? The thought didn't bother her. They were just outside her window, patrolling the quiet suburban forest, protecting her—

"Take it from the top, Bone Daddy!" a ghoul yelled from the bar, so loud it pierced right through her bedroom wall on the second story. Chortles and drunken applause followed as the organ and the saxophone smashed together into a torrid matrimony of noise, followed by howls from all present.

Jolted awake, Sadiyeh sank back into bed, feeling terribly lonely all of a sudden.

"Would you like me to tell them to quiet down?" Midway asked gently from her corner.

Sadiyeh shook her head, fighting to keep the tears at bay. That wasn't what hurt. "I'm used to their singing. It's fine."

* * *

The only Rioter who still terrified Sadiyeh was Connor Bailey.

He had a habit of grabbing her shoulder when her back was turned. She could never hear the tall, fleet-footed Lupinite coming. It didn't matter where she was, at the Blackstone Hotel or out and about in the streets of Chicago—he would sneak up on her, grabbing her with a death grip.

Ignoring her yelp of surprise, he'd whisper dangerously low in her ear: "Eight days," or "Three a.m.," or "Ya got five minutes, love." His face would break into a demonic grin before he'd loosen his grip and go about his day. Sometimes when she'd see him with Gushiken, he'd give her a death glare when his husband wasn't looking before quickly turning it into a polite wave or bow and move on.

"He's just messing with you," Maria said after Sadiyeh told her of the incidents. They were at the office kitchen counter, huddled together for privacy.

"You sure?" Sadiyeh said.

"Oh, he's done it to everyone, even me. If he finds someone especially soft and cuddly, he keeps at it a bit longer because he finds them more fun to mess with, I guess. It isn't as much fun if the person gives as good as they get."

"So I'm an easy target? Great." She recalled Gushiken informing her, cigarette in hand, that they could smell the fear on her.

Maria giggled and gave her a soothing pat. "Maybe you remind him of his sister."

"Really? Then why would he…"

"Ah, I forgot, you didn't grow up with siblings. Maybe he misses the days when he could play around with his sister before she fell sick."

Sadiyeh sighed. That didn't make her feel any better. "I wish I could speak to Gushiken about this."

"And tell him what? To put a leash on his husband?"

The two women giggled, and at that very moment, Gushiken emerged from the elevator, husband in tow. That only made them laugh harder, drawing confused glances from the two before they turned back to their business.

Sadiyeh prepared herself for Bailey after that, turning a scare moment into small talk, catching him off guard whenever she could. She even brought him and his sister treats. The look on his face was worthy of a photo. However, she much preferred it if they didn't cross paths at all. It was a futile wish, as the Lupinite could materialize out of nowhere. She would just have to keep disarming him with kindness.

* * *

Friday, September 12, 893 NE
Sadiyeh left her day shift and stepped into a city that had gone grey with a heavy rainstorm the likes of which hadn't been seen

in years. She reached into her sling bag, but of course she didn't have her umbrella.

I really need to start watching the news again, Sadiyeh thought. *At least the weather forecast.*

She cast a repelling spell around herself, but the wind broke through her shield, drenching her to the bone. An umbrella would have been just as futile.

She looked at the tall buildings around her. Many of them had lost power. The wind whistled loudly and blew at such speeds she needed to hold on to a lamppost. She shouldn't have even come out here. Visibility was nonexistent; it was a miracle that she could even take a couple of steps.

I'll just weather the storm, she thought. *Or find a place to shelter for the next hour or so.*

Using the lampposts as markers, she trudged from one to another, mapping out her way through the city.

The wind roared again, and she ducked down low, placing her center of gravity in one area so she wouldn't get swept away. When she rose to her feet again, someone or something clasped her elbow.

Unable to open her eyes, Sadiyeh couldn't tell what or who it was. She tried to move when the pressure grew against her.

"Come here, sweetheart."

She didn't recognize the voice. Was it one of Gushiken's men? The hand gripped her tightly, tugging her against the wind's current. Then she felt it. Another hand. Copping a feel.

Before she could do anything, she heard a growl behind her: "We won' be havin' any of dat!"

The hands tore away from her as a scream pierced the night,

swallowed by the wind and a wolf's howl. She thought she felt something warm and wet splatter over her.

Then another pair of hands was on her, this time grabbing her shoulder.

"Dis way."

It was Bailey.

Shaking like a wet leaf, Sadiyeh followed him blindly into the front seat of a car. He slipped behind the wheel and drove off. She sat there, drenched, mute, cowering in a corner, afraid of what would happen next. She tried not to stare at the blood dripping from his canines and that on her own dress.

She could barely make out the streets he drove through, and in her state, she barely had time to marvel at Bailey's expertise navigating through the storm. The next thing she knew, Bailey was escorting her up black-and-gold ceramic steps to a penthouse—one of a couple he owned in the city. She took in the black porcelain vases, art deco paintings, and a pair of ornate candelabras before he whisked her off into a room.

He informed her that they would be spending the night here as he ran her a bath in his exquisite claw-foot tub.

"Ya're about her size," he said, tossing a robe and dress at her. He turned on his heel and left the bathroom before Sadiyeh could find her voice to thank him.

She called to update Brian and Midway of her situation, then washed and dried herself. She could hear Bailey on the phone with Gushiken, undoubtedly informing him of the incident. Craning her neck, she went to peek at him behind the wall. He stood before the floor-to-ceiling window of the living room, one hand in his pocket, the other tensely gripping his phone. The storm raged on, with occasional streaks of lightning flashing across the dim room. Although she could not make out what he was saying, she heard hints of anger and grief in his voice.

"Are you okay?"

The timid voice made Sadiyeh jump.

A small, thin woman sat up in bed; Sadiyeh had missed her, having sneaked past the bedroom to spy on Bailey. The young woman had long dark wispy hair and the same grey eyes as Bailey.

"Oh, sorry!" Sadiyeh said and bowed. "Um, are you Finley Bailey?"

Finley's face brightened. "My brother's mentioned me to you?"

Sadiyeh nodded. "He did. He might have passed along some of my treats to you."

"Th-that was you? Thank you! I've really appreciated them!"

Sadiyeh smiled. "I'm Sadiyeh. Sadiyeh Mhalabiyeh."

Finley gasped. "You're that writer?! I love your books!"

She weakly lifted an arm, motioning to her bookshelves. "Connor's been getting me your stuff! I want to read them all, but I don't think he knows which ones I don't have. He's always so busy. It makes him scatterbrained and forgetful!"

Sadiyeh glimpsed the titles.

He didn't get the Hikmat books, at least, she thought approvingly.

There were a number of other trinkets in Finley's room, and she was more than happy to give Sadiyeh a tour. Many were from Gushiken, and the thought of how much the jewelry, porcelain dolls, and other gifts must have cost made Sadiyeh dizzy.

"Oh—and look at this!" Finley said with a giggle after opening an album. "I begged and begged Tetsu to get this for me—Connor doesn't know! I made Tetsu promise!"

She handed over a photo to Sadiyeh. She recognized him as one of the Lupinite lieutenants, young but powerfully built. The thought of Finley asking the patriarch to get his photo… Sadiyeh couldn't suppress her giggle.

"You two would make an adorable couple," she said.

Finley's eyes shone. "His name's Eddie Maxwell. I wanted to write him a love letter, but I'm not sure what to say."

Sadiyeh studied the photo again. *Bailey just saved my life*, she thought. *It's the least I can do to repay him.*

"I can help you," she said. "I've never written a love letter personally, but my characters have written plenty."

"You'll help me? *Really?*"

Sadiyeh nodded. "Of course."

* * *

Later that night, Sadiyeh woke up with a start. Finley slept peacefully next to her, the completed love letter tucked safely beneath her pillow where Bailey wouldn't find it.

Sadiyeh slipped out, careful not to wake Finley. She saw that Bailey was out on the balcony.

The storm must have stopped sometime during the night. Bailey leaned heavily against the rails and looked out across the Chicago skyline, nursing a glass of whiskey and with a cigarette tucked between two fingers. City lights twinkled in his forlorn gaze.

Sadiyeh approached him with small, tentative steps.

"Hey, Sad," he said in a tone she hadn't heard before. Neither sardonic nor filled with his usual strength and wit. Melancholic? "Get back inside, ya'll catch yer death."

"I'm sorry I kept you away from your husband," Sadiyeh said.

"'Tis arright," Bailey said. "Not the first time we slept apart. Ya get used to it."

"Um, I heard you speaking with him earlier…"

A brief smile tugged on Bailey's face. "Gotta a mess for 'im to clean up."

"Oh."

So the guy was dead. She didn't want to think what would have happened had Bailey not stepped in, had he not happened to be around. Still, the fact remained that a fellow human had died at the hands of the Riot…

"Thank you for saving my life," Sadiyeh said. She bowed lightly.

"Ya met Finley."

"Yes, she's lovely and sweet." Sadiyeh glanced around, unsure what to say that wouldn't anger him. She didn't dare to mention the love letter.

"She's a sweet li'l 'ing. I'd wipe the whole city dead if anything ever happened to her."

Unsure how to reply to that, Sadiyeh simply nodded. Bailey turned back to continue gazing out into the city.

She expected him to start teasing her again at any moment,

remembering what Maria had said about her reminding Bailey of Finley, but Bailey seemed to be lost in his own troubled thoughts. His eyes appeared bloodshot, and she wondered if he spent nights weeping over Finley's condition in the safety of this place, away from Gushiken or anyone's prodding.

Sadiyeh had never seen this side of Bailey before, and it almost broke her heart.

"*Yo*—get back inside! Or ya wan' me help ya catch your death?!"

Almost.

* * *

New Year's Eve, 893 NE
"Wait, so you were first sworn in as the patriarch on Halloween, twenty-one years ago," Maria said, face set in concentration as she tinkered with something on her phone. "That was… October 31 of 872! That was on a Blue Moon!"

"Was it?" Gushiken asked, amusement in his voice.

Sadiyeh sat next to Maria on the velvet couch, listening in with amusement. Adjacent to them were Gushiken and Bailey, who had lit their cigarettes by touching the tips together, an act that shouldn't have sent tingles down Sadiyeh's spine the way it did.

Gushiken had reserved several floors of the Blackstone Hotel for their office party, for all the workers of Iridium Bay Publishing, its clients, and of course his own family. The space included a couple of conference suites, the arcade, the bar, and even the swimming pool.

How far she had come since exactly one year ago. How lonely she'd been, how full of despair. The world wasn't getting any better out there, but at least she could get away from it all whenever she stepped into the Blackstone Hotel.

She watched as her fellow Moonchildren reveled in the final hours of the year. Mobster Lupinites morphed into their wolf forms and got into brawls as onlookers cheered them on; then they'd pop back into their human forms, laughing and patting one another on the back, completely oblivious to any cuts and bruises they'd earned in the fight. So far, Maxwell was winning every time he engaged in a fight, perhaps in hopes of earning himself a word or two of praise from Gushiken.

"Yes!" Maria cried out drunkenly. She showed Gushiken a calendar on her phone. "It was a Blue Moon that night! You know what this means?! You should call your family Blue Moon Riot!"

"Blue Moon Riot?" Gushiken said and leaned toward his husband. "Has a nice ring to it. What do you think, love?"

Bailey shrugged. "I'd rather name it after ya." That earned him a kiss below the ear. Sadiyeh tried not to stare.

"You'll always be remembered as the first patriarch!" Maria said. "But think of it this way: whenever people think of Blue Moons, whenever anyone says the name, they'll quiver in their shoes! Their immediate thought will be your family. You're leaving behind a legacy! I mean, that *is* your plan, isn't it? Have you thought about an heir?"

"Not really..." Gushiken said, frowning. "But I've made no plans to bite the dust anytime soon."

Sadiyeh tuned out that conversation and tuned into another. Talks between Rioters about their other businesses carried over, and Sadiyeh could hear snippets of what else the family was involved in: casinos, construction work, bars, taxis, music and acting, and seedier places she didn't wish to know about.

"Why not go into medicine?" Maria asked Gushiken, diverting Sadiyeh's attention back to them. "You have a foot in nearly every aspect—oh, I know! Open up a pharmacy!"

Gushiken laughed. "We'd need someone with the brains."

Maria poured him another drink, leaning so close to him, it was a miracle Bailey didn't try to pry her off his mate. *"Think of all the money you could rake in, Tetsu!"*

"Am I the mob boss, or you?"

Elsewhere, Russell was being hounded by one of the Lupinite lieutenants.

"From what I understand, the Magi carries the surname of the mother."

"That's correct," Russell said. "In honor of the Moon Mother and the Daughters of the Moon."

"Why only the mother?" the lieutenant demanded.

"Yeah, are men seen as useless?!" another Lupinite called out. Sadiyeh recalled his surname being Adams.

"Desmonites go by clan names…most of the time!" one of the other editors, Barthélémy Rougeux, interjected. He was flaxen haired, pale, and rather small in stature compared to the other men, and his cheeks remained pale regardless of how much he drank.

"Lupinites will agree on a surname regardless of gender," the first lieutenant said. "How do you even decide when the matter is between two women or gender-neutral parents or—"

"Why are you asking me? I didn't make the rules!" Russel cried out.

Sadiyeh grinned into her warm nonalcoholic drink. She spotted the Desmonite photographer, whose named she had since learned was Myskia Nyborg, perched gracefully above a painting, eyeing Bailey intently. Catching Sadiyeh's gaze, they gave her a wink, then turned into a bat, swept down, and stole Bailey's drink right from his hand.

* * *

The new year saw Sadiyeh embark on a new project.

She took to the library inside Murklins Manor, reading up on the criminal syndicates of old: Italian mafias, Japanese yakuza, Russian *bratvas*, Chinese *triads*, Middle Eastern *baltagiya*.

This earned her judgmental looks from the mummy librarian, but Sadiyeh brushed them away with a wave of her hand.

"All good research for my next book!"

Nefertiti shook her head and tugged her wispy shawl tighter around herself. "I would be careful about romanticizing them."

"I'm not romanticizing! It's important to know all I can—the good, the bad, and the ugly."

"You still wish to write a story about them."

"That doesn't mean I—"

She had to admit to herself she did trust Gushiken's men a lot more than she trusted the police on the street, but that did not mean she thought of them as angels—really!

* * *

Russell came rushing into the office, eyes wide.

"Oh, shit!" he hissed to Maria and Sadiyeh. "I just saw Bailey drag one of the family. Guy looks wrecked!"

"Russell, you know we shouldn't eavesdrop," Maria said. "What're they saying, Rougeux?"

Her fellow editor turned into a bat and flew toward the door but immediately flew back.

"Act natural," he said.

The door burst open again, and the Lupinites filed out, with the beaten-up Lupinite concealed somewhere within their ranks, either for protection…or so that no one could catch a glimpse of him.

Everyone in the office worked quietly, pretending nothing was amiss, as the family had passed by millions of times before. Once they left through the elevator, Rougeux made his move again, searching through the office and then popping back out as a bat.

"Nothing weird in there," he said. "Looks like they dragged the kid to the back alley!"

Sadiyeh couldn't stay in her seat. Adams, that was the young Lupinite's surname. She remembered how much fun he had had during the New Year's celebration.

She joined her friends as they pressed themselves against the glass, trying to see what was going.

Out in the alley, Adams had been stripped of his clothes. Fresh wounds marred his back. The Lupinites morphed back into their human forms and took their spots around Gushiken, who was busy loading his gun.

"Please, boss! Let me explain myself!"

"We don't take well to informers," Gushiken said gravely.

Sadiyeh kept staring even as the others looked away.

* * *

"Doesn't it ever scare you?" Sadiyeh asked Myskia Nyborg, the Desmonite photographer. They kept their voices hushed as they walked down old Michigan Avenue. They had run into each another after work, and Sadiyeh couldn't help but pour out her heart to Myskia about what she'd witnessed of that poor doomed Lupinite.

Myskia gave a half-hearted shrug as the early spring wind blew their dark bangs against their eyes. "The family has to protect itself. If someone goes traitor—"

"They have a strict code not to hurt any Moonchild!"

"Perhaps not you and me, unless we cross a line. They're actually quite strict with one another. Gotta keep an eye on your dogs, or they'll go loose. I hear Gushiken can get as tough on them as he does with the Earthchildren clients."

"Yeah, I've heard stories of how they've treated some of their clients…and even other businesses."

"You don't seem happy at all."

"It's just…they can be so cruel." Sadiyeh had halted the research on her new book idea since that incident. She still thought of it from time to time, drawn by the romantic image she had built of the main character, but the thought of what Gushiken had willingly done to one of his own men…

"How else do we get paid?" Myskia said. "We all need money to live. You can't just live on passion alone."

"True, but—"

"You know, I was dropped by my former agency because one of my photos had the night sky in it. The night sky! The Moon was just barely a crescent! And if that doesn't boil your blood, then you'd better believe me when I tell you this: other photographers have gotten their shit published with the exact same subjects at no penalty. Especially if they're flattering photos of United Domain members."

"What?" The thought of Gordon going against his word left a cold pit in her stomach.

"You heard me!" Myskia fished out their phone and handed it to Sadiyeh. "Look at these photos! All from the same photographer! Always of the same politicians. None of the Elite, for some reason—not like we ever see their faces anyway—but look! The Moon, the stars, in each of them! And I was told I couldn't publish my damn book for the exact same reason!"

"Betcha it's 'cause I'm a Moonchild.

"The law is flawed. It's biased. It's mainly there to silence us Moonchildren and a few others. So yeah, from where I'm standing, let Gushiken charge the non-Moonies however he wants. Let him ruffle a few feathers here and there. Let there be suffering on both sides! It evens out the playing field. If one of our own steps out of line, then that's on them."

Sadiyeh stared out over the river. *And with that, we've reached the muddy middle.*

"Ya know what I wanted to do before I turned to photography?"

Sadiyeh shook her head.

"Medical work," Myskia said. They stopped at the Michigan Avenue Bridge and peered out at the Chicago River. "It's part of a Desmonite's natural Moon-given abilities. Well, for some of us, at least. We have this gift where we can suck all the blood out of a person, then return it, having fully cleansed their blood in our bodies. We rid the blood of any diseases found in it, but this only works on blood. Can't do anything about scars or an infection, nothing like that. And if you do that to a Lupinite? You can make them stronger. Or so the rumor goes.

"Anyway, try getting *that* accepted by the rest of the world. It looks terrifying to the uninformed. We look like monsters, leeching blood and life out of a person. So yeah, I never got accepted into medical school."

"There isn't a school for your kind of practice?" Sadiyeh asked.

Myskia scoffed. "Ya think we have the numbers, money, and resources as Lupinites? Out of all the Moonchildren, Desmonites have the tiniest population! I'm just thankful I have someplace with Gushiken."

Sadiyeh sighed heavily. "Yeah…"

* * *

Branded with Love.

That was the title Sadiyeh had settled on for her mobster novel. Despite her persistent feeling of unease toward the Lupinites and her desire to tuck away the novel into the labyrinth of her imagination, she could not deny that the story still captivated her—perhaps even more so now with the complexities she understood of the family.

On the monorail rides to and from the lab, and at times

when work stretched into a long, dull monotonous din of code work and feeding paper into a machine, her imagination carried her away to the more exciting and thrilling world of a mobster legend.

Her usual humor barely made an appearance in this novel; instead, the prose dripped with sensuality, each sentence crafted to elicit one dark and hidden emotion after another, sparked by the farthest depths of her own id. The main character was dark and mysterious and deadly and deeply sexual—everything she loved about Gushiken but would never openly confess. He did things to elicit love and respect from those around him; he did things to elicit fear and anger from those around him. Sadiyeh wanted to bear it all: the gritty, complex world of the Lupinites.

In the novel, the main character's love interest wasn't a woman. Sadiyeh didn't care that the ever-preceptive Maria would draw the comparisons between the main character and Gushiken and either tease Sadiyeh or become heartbroken. It just didn't seem right any other way.

The lover was a man, green to the criminal underworld but one who would be taken under the wing of this mastermind, saved in the nick of time during a nasty brawl. He would be forged into a champion of the underground by the mob boss. There would be genuine love between them, but the boss was ready, ever so ready, to kill him without hesitation.

A few times, Sadiyeh almost stopped writing the novel, wondering what would happen if Gushiken read it and saw the similarities. Or Bailey.

"Ooh, this is very different, Sadiyeh!" Maria said over the

phone when she was done going through the manuscript. "Were you thinking of using a pseudonym?"

Sadiyeh thought for a moment before declining.

Gushiken and Bailey were going to find out eventually. Why hide this?

* * *

Friday, January 28, 896 NE
"Dat made for quite a riveting read, love," Bailey teased Sadiyeh the next time he saw her after *Branded with Love*'s publication. Her eyes widened. His canines shone with his wicked grin. "Stunnin' research! Beautiful writing! Felt I was right there! Quite inspired, if I may say. Not sure if I should let Finley read it, though, if ya know what I mean."

Face red and flushed all over, Sadiyeh dashed out of the office. She couldn't bear to tell him, nor Maria, that she had planned on writing two more novels from that universe.

* * *

Saturday, July 27, 898 NE
"Who's that out there, ya reckon?" one zombie asked another. A tiny crowd formed around a window as ghouls of all walks of unlife strained to get a glimpse of the newcomer approaching Murklins Manor.

A ghost wearing a formal suit and monocle drew up to the window and announced in a loud, exaggeratedly posh voice: "Healthy, warm skin intact and smooth, no missing bones or eyes, sweet lips untouched by any worm bite—she is a living, breathing woman!"

Groans rippled through the crowd.

"Really, guys?!" Sadiyeh said as she ran past them. "How rude! That's my guest!"

Maria Vine stood a few yards away from Murklins Manor, looking tall and lovely in a long skirt and a pointy hat that cast a long shadow in the early summer evening.

"Maria! Happy birthday!" Sadiyeh called as she ran out.

"Sadiyeh!" Maria greeted her with a hug. "So glad you invited me over!"

"Yeah, well…just don't tell Gushiken or Bailey—or any of their men—where I live," she said. "And…not Russell either, just to be on the safe side."

"Of course not!" Maria winked and bowed in a playful manner. "And you don't go telling Russell I'm working when I should be celebrating!"

Sadiyeh chuckled sheepishly. "Deal."

"There! We both have secrets to keep!"

"It's not only that," Sadiyeh said as she led Maria inside. "The place is more than just a sanctuary for the undead. This is a hotel. The owner raised me since I was a baby, and I reside in a small portion of the manor. I don't want any trouble here."

"You have my word!" Maria said with a bow. "You've lived here for how long?"

"All my life," Sadiyeh said. "My mothers placed me on the doorstep before vanishing off to Moon Mother-knows-where. Brian and the others took care of me. I've rented my quarters ever since I could work. I really should get my own place; it feels a bit odd living next to the undead here. But...it's the only place I've ever called home."

Brian and Midway stood near the entrance, ready to welcome the women inside. Brian had already teased Sadiyeh about finally bringing home a prospective partner, and Midway had supported the idea, but Sadiyeh was quick to shoot it down.

"Why don't you first focus on successfully wooing the librarian?" she had teased Brian.

Seeing Maria in person, Brian's bony face held a considerable expression of pain, as though it hurt him that Sadiyeh was passing this lovely Magi up. The ever so loyal Midway's expression remained impassive, but Sadiyeh sensed a similar sentiment.

Over the years, as her little crush on Gushiken had ebbed, her love for Maria had only grown. But she didn't dare to mention that to Brian. He was rather old fashioned and would certainly push her toward marriage at the first chance, and Sadiyeh wasn't ready for that. She was already in a committed relationship with her writing. However, while writing might have been Sadiyeh's first love, she dreamed of Maria frequently, and she missed her if she went for weeks or months without seeing her, as she was wont to do when deep in draft writing or revisions.

Nevertheless, this wasn't the reason for Maria being here.

"A skeleton and an android," Maria giggled. "They make quite a pair. Our past and our future!"

Sadiyeh nodded, blushing a little. "Midway will be leaving next week. She's helped me a lot."

"Ah, that's wonderful to hear!" Maria ran up and shook Midway's hands. "Pleasure to finally meet you!"

"A pleasure as well, Ms. Vine," Midway said, giving Sadiyeh a wink over Maria's shoulder: *Don't pass her up.*

Brian led them to the dining room, where a magnificent feast awaited them. Franklin had wanted to take his dinner elsewhere out of respect, but they insisted on him staying.

"Do forgive my improper state of dress," he said.

"You're fine!" Maria squeaked as she sized him up.

The food itself—filet mignon and herbed mashed potatoes—earned a cry of delight from Maria.

"Okay, but you have to let me take a sample for Russie!" she said. "I'll just tell him we dined at some fancy place where the food was amazing but the customer service was horrible. I'm taking all the lemon cheesecake for myself!"

"Sure," Sadiyeh giggled.

They tucked into their meal, enjoying a nice conversation that consisted mainly of Maria asking Franklin about his life as a chimeric being and the sort of work he did as a woodchopper.

"Would you build me a cabin in any part of the woods?" Maria asked. "There's this patch higher up in the Northeast American Domains that are just lovely during the fall!"

Franklin sighed. "I very much do not enjoy traveling at my age, but for you I will, Maria."

"You're a darling!"

After dinner, Sadiyeh led Maria to the study on the second floor. Midway stood waiting for them beside a bookcase where some books hummed; a few preened their neighbors like birds. Maria marveled over them for a while.

"How adorable!" she said. "Do you write here?"

"Mostly in my room," Sadiyeh said. "But I do come here

occasionally. There's also a big library on the first floor, but I can't take you there. The librarian prefers not seeing too many living nonresident guests there. I think she just doesn't want to be seen."

"Why so? Was she someone important during her life?"

"You could say that."

They settled by the window, poring over Sadiyeh's most recent manuscript, titled *Bloodbored*. Midway busied herself by pouring them some tea, then motioned for the humming books to keep it down.

"'Fess up," Maria said teasingly, tapping the pages. "You were inspired by Myskia, weren't you?"

Sadiyeh couldn't help but retreat shyly; it was the way Maria studied her, large eyes so intently peering into her soul.

"You can't hide, Sadiyeh! I see how you two have become friends over the years!"

"Yes," Sadiyeh admitted. No point in hiding the truth. The idea of a Desmonite causally saving people by sucking their blood while Earthchildren watched in horror was just too tempting. A story with a misunderstood hero. A story containing hilarity and irony but also some heartwarming moments. Exactly her sort of thing.

Maria threw her head back as she laughed. "I knew it! And I just *knew* Gushiken was the inspiration for the *Branded* series—I mean, come on! A sexy Lupinite mobster?"

Sadiyeh covered her face in her hands. If *Branded with Love* wasn't telling enough, then its sequel, *Branded for Life*, certainly was.

"That obvious, huh?" she said in a tiny voice. "He doesn't know, does he?"

"I don't think he has time to read," Maria said, which helped quell Sadiyeh's nerves. "His husband, on the other hand…"

"Don't remind me."

"Oh, *peesh*! You haven't been at the office during the week! Bailey *loves* them! I'm sure he's used a few of the scenes in the second book as inspiration for the bedroom!"

"Maria!"

Coughing out some of her butterfly pea flower tea, Sadiyeh grabbed the manuscript and pretended to read with extreme attention, hiding her face behind the sheets of white paper.

"You're the one who came up with those positions, Sad!"

"I am not listening to you!"

Sadiyeh could swear that the entire room twinkled with Maria's jubilance. That had to be her special magic.

"Aw, you're blushing," Maria cooed. "You're so cute when you're flustered!" She slid a hand under the manuscripts and caressed Sadiyeh's face. Before Sadiyeh knew it, soft lips brushed against her cheeks, then moved to her lips. Sadiyeh gasped at the kiss before melting into it, glad that the manuscript hid her face from Midway.

"Got my birthday present," Maria said softly and winked before straightening her back. "Hey, let's toast to Gushiken and his Riot!"

Sadiyeh, still a bit dazed but grinning from ear to ear, nodded and raised her mug. "In light of all the new stupid laws the United Domains have been passing!"

"Oh, yes!"

"To Blue Moon Riot and to Patriarch Tetsu Gushiken, for

keeping the Moonchildren afloat every time the big guys try to sink us!"

In the years since signing on with Iridium Bay Publishing, Sadiyeh had authored several more books, such as the long-awaited sequel to *Grapes for Apes* and *Carrots for Parrots*, titled *Melons for Felons*. The series of books now had a name: *These Nuts May Vary*, which caused Maria to fall off her chair in a great fit of glee the moment she saw it. She had shrieked so loud that some Rioters had run in to see what the commotion was about.

Sadiyeh had also begun a new series, a bit darker in tone but still carrying her typical wit, known as *The Deadly Gin Trilogy*. *Gin Glass Heroes* and *Gin & Toxin* were the first two in the series, and she had a bit more research to do before starting on the third. This was Russell's favorite of her newer works.

With the spike in her productivity ever since breaking away from OakFinch Press, she'd revisited older and unfinished manuscripts and breathed new life into them. Every day brought her new ideas. She ventured more through Chicago, lost in her thoughts; she researched extensively and dreamed long into the night.

"So…when are you gonna write a book based on me?" Maria asked with a flick of her hair.

"I already have a book with a Magi protagonist—*The Deadly Gin Trilogy*."

"No, I meant *me*! When do I get to be your muse? Myskia gets to be the star of *Bloodbored*!" Lowing her voice, Maria added, "Do you find your girlfriend boring?"

Sadiyeh laughed. "No, of course not! We'll see. I just need to think about you more deeply, I guess."

"You mean you don't think about me?!"

Sadiyeh's face burned. "I-I do! I just…don't know where to take you, as a character."

Maria made a grand show of being offended before her lips curled into a smirk. "Make me a villainess. No, like—make me the protagonist! A nasty, evil woman, with lots of money! But! Make the story in *my* point of view, got that? I want to be the villain *and* the protagonist! Make me compelling. A baddie, but really complex! Oh, and—and! Dig deep into my psyche as I struggle with my morals and decide to help the hero in the end! Make it so that no one will know whether to hate me or root for me!"

"I'll see what I can think of." Sadiyeh lifted her mug of tea and took a long sip. The truth was, she wanted a story inspired by Maria to be something very special, just like with Amneh and the children's storybook, and that made for a creative block.

"Do you get the chance to read Sadiyeh's stories as she works on them?" Maria asked Midway, who booted back up at the question.

"Sometimes, yes," Midway said with a bow. "Once Sad gets into the zone, the entire universe ceases to exist. Sometimes I hear her talk endlessly about it in her sleep."

"How adorable!" Maria teased. "So! Any thoughts on a book inspired by Midway?" Maria turned to Sadiyeh as she motioned toward the android.

Sadiyeh frowned. Now that Maria had brought it up,

leaving Midway out felt rather rude. "Not really. I've mostly wanted to get stories out there about the Moonchildren."

"Fair enough."

Midway perked up at that. "But, Sad, your current project—"

"I know," Sadiyeh said quickly, but Maria pounced at the opportunity.

"What new project?" she asked.

"Pay attention to the manuscript, Maria!"

"What new project?"

Sadiyeh sighed. "I haven't thought of a name yet, but I was considering writing something about…waterpeople. Merpeople, people of Atlantis. I haven't quite made up my mind."

She got up and crossed the room to a wide expanse of wall. With a wave of her hand, she began drawing a family tree, starting with one word in the top center: Moon Mother. Twelve lines branched from the name.

"We know so little of the Moon mythos," Sadiyeh said. "Yet somehow we know there were twelve Daughters of the Moon. We know that Desmonites protected the skies, Lupinites protected the lands, and the Magi protected everyone from the spirit world. It only makes sense that there were Moonchildren who protected the oceans."

"I can see that!" Maria said. "And you think Atlantis was their city?"

"I'm only going by the stories we already have," Sadiyeh said, "but it makes sense, doesn't it? Land, skies, sea, aether… where else could they be?"

"And now we're probably cut off from them," Maria mused. "The Floods came and drowned so many cities. Good for the merfolk, I guess. More places to live. But for us…" She studied the tree for a few long moments before continuing, "And what of the other branches? What other Mooncousins could we possibly have? Centaurs? Fawns?"

"I've wondered about that too," Sadiyeh said. "What if they are not human at all?"

"What do you mean?"

"Our myths are full of other beings. Elves, dwarves, maybe even jinn…what if they too are Moonchildren?"

Maria rubbed her lower lip with a thumb. "Huh. What do you suppose happened to them?"

"That's my question. I asked patrons at the bar, the ones who were around during the Old Era. Some don't even think elves and dwarves ever existed."

"Then maybe that's your answer."

"No…but then…the stories." She glanced back up at the tree. "Their stories exist alongside stories of werewolves and witches and vampires. Cultures from around the world, even late into the Old Era, spoke of the 'the unseen' or 'hidden' people and respected them in their everyday life. J. R. R. Tolkien's works speak of them so vividly that I wonder if he had the chance to speak with them."

"Tolkien?! Ah, come on! We have different versions of his notes! Those are only stories!"

"The same way my stories, based on real people, have many different drafts? I tell stories about the Moonchildren, hoping to preserve their memory in case we disappear. Perhaps Tolkien and others like him tried to preserve something too."

Maria paused. "I—ah, I see what you mean."

"And there's the case of my mothers," Sadiyeh said. "Wherever did they go? What if they were searching for the land of Faerie? What if that's where they are now? Maybe that's why no one's heard from them for all these years!" The alternative explanation, something to do with the United Domains, was too horrifying to entertain.

Picking up her prized pen, Sadiyeh conjured up Muse. The tall figure leaned over her expectantly, loyally. She smiled up at them.

"Hey," she said in a voice only they could hear. "I've been thinking…about the lesser-known Moonchildren. Got a new idea I want to store."

* * *

Maria gasped, unable to pry her eyes away from Muse.

"She's been conversing with Muse more and more often," Midway said. "I think she confines in them more than she does me these days."

Maria cleared her throat. She had never seen any magic like that before.

Chapter 4

On a Dark and Stormy Night

Wednesday, September 3, 899 NE

Rain pelted fast and heavy that evening. Sadiyeh clung tightly to her umbrella with one hand as the other gripped the handle on the pedestrian overpass, fighting against a heavy current so strong she could barely keep her eyes open.

A loud whistle pierced the air. For a moment she passed it off as the storm, but it came again, accompanied by shouts. Sadiyeh snapped to attention, quickly growing aware of her surroundings. The howling wind carried the sound of anguished cries.

"Leon! Bobbie! Agu! *Hurry!*"

Was that Tora?

"Janssen! Dante! Möbius! *Dis way!*"

Bailey?

Sadiyeh looked around and spotted the crowd a few paces behind her. Some of them were huddled very close together, and as they passed Sadiyeh, she understood why when she got a good look at the man they were carrying.

Tetsu Gushiken. At first, she barely recognized him, but there he was: pale and unconscious, bloodied from head to toe, clothes torn and dirtied. Drops of blood mingled with the rain, streaking the pavement below.

Sadiyeh's grip on the umbrella loosened. Her heart plummeted. A great gust of wind passed and blew the umbrella right out of her hands, but Sadiyeh didn't turn to fetch it, staring instead, open mouthed and drenched, at the scene that she had just witnessed.

* * *

"How is he?"

Sadiyeh had chased down the crowd carrying Gushiken, led by Bailey and some Riot and Nine Knives members, to St. Mercy University Hospital in downtown Chicago. It was a lot more prestigious than the small community hospital Sadiyeh had been brought to years prior, but the sterile smell, white bed linen, and beeping from numerous vitals monitors were all the same.

Standing here brought back bittersweet memories for Sadiyeh: the pain and numbness that had led her to the doors of the emergency room, then the odd ecstatic joy, the spark of an idea that ended her ties with one company only to find another…

She could sense the ghosts who lingered here, those trapped in the walls of the hospital, and shivered at the thought of a similar fate befalling Gushiken.

She needed to sit down.

Bailey gazed out the floor-to-ceiling window of the fifth floor at the pouring rain, lost in his thoughts. A large bruise bloomed under his left eye.

"Critical," he replied to her question. "But da medics don' believe his condition will worsen."

Conditions can always fluctuate, Sadiyeh thought, recalling how Midway had been appointed to remain by her side. Her loving, loyal android companion had only left Murklins Manor last year, her services no longer required. Granted, Sadiyeh's and Gushiken's situations were different. Perhaps Gushiken would make a full recovery after all. But wasn't the human body (and mind) unpredictable?

She struggled for the right words to say.

"Um…how…did it happen?"

"Some punks kidnapped a pup. One of our men saw da whole incident and reported it to us. Dey were ready to mess him up…at the very least. He couldn' have been more than five years."

Sadiyeh slowly nodded. Only the Lupinite mobsters called their own young "pups," which she found both endearing and a bit odd.

"Tetsu wasn' gonna turn his back on him. You know what he's like toward the Moonies. So he got into a scuffle. It bled out into da streets. There was chase dat led us to da harbor. Turned into an all-out brawl between us and da other gang. Tetsu wasn' abou' to give up without getting da pup back. Turned beastly in da heat of battle. In da end, he ate a few rounds of bullets. Both da human and wolf parts of him were gravely wounded. Da bastards ran off, and we carried him here. Some of our men fared a lot worse."

"W-worse?"

Bailey nodded. "Milton Rost. Abram Petrov. Eddie Maxwell. All dead."

An icy shiver ran down Sadiyeh's spine. Petrov, the Lupinite who had driven Sadiyeh and Garrett away from the protests. Rost, one of the younger Lupinites Sadiyeh had had fun watching fighting at the office's annual New Year's Eve parties.

And Maxwell. Finley's Eddie Maxwell…

Sadiyeh's eyes welled with tears, and with them came memories of helping Finley with that love letter many years ago. Of sitting next to Maria and watching Finley, so radiant in her dress, marry Eddie a couple of years later. After many failed tries, Finley was due with their first child in just a few months…

"Poor fuckers. Have no time to give dem proper burials. Gonna have to turn them to ash before da pigs come sniffing around our hideouts."

Sadiyeh nodded again, her hands numb and cold over her knees.

Something stirred deep in her core, a ghost from the past she thought had been swept away with the sands of time.

"Da pup is fine, in case ya're wondering."

Sadiyeh struggled to speak. Each movement felt faint… as though it were happening to someone else far away. "Ah… good."

Bailey glanced back. "Dey better update me on his progress, I got somewhere to be. Future of da family's at stake…"

Sadiyeh startled but immediately covered it up, trying to

not to show that she had heard Bailey. She hung her head, an icy feeling of dread threatening to consume her from within.

She hadn't realized just how good she'd had it all these years. Under the unrelenting oppression wrought by the United Domains, there existed a little bubble of freedom, and Gushiken was its creator. So many relied on him. Though he was not a sinless man, he was good to them. He was their deliverance in the dark, a symbol of comfort and stability in their lives.

And now he was dying.

Had she taken it all for granted? Had they all? How long was this family going to last?

Her fingernails dug into her palms.

Gushiken and his men had done so much to protect them all, Moonchildren and Earthchildren alike. Should he be taken away, should all of this be taken away…she could not bear the thought of plummeting back to that same darkness, hitting roadblock after roadblock, trying to live under the constraints of that society, contending with an endlessly cruel and oppressive government, not back there in that dark place, that—

"Sadiyeh?"

Bailey's voice came very softly. One of his hands swept around her shoulder, and the other rested gently on her arm. She hadn't realized that she was trembling. His eyes studied her, shining with a gentleness she was unaccustomed to from the Riot's underboss.

She wanted to kick herself. *Don't trouble him! He's going through enough!*

"I'm sorry," she whispered. "I'm just shocked. He always seemed invincible."

Bailey gave a sad chuckle. "In our line of work, it's only a matter of time before injury or death gets us."

"Don't say that! I can't lose either of you!"

"Don' be afraid, Sad. Tetsu isn' going anywhere—*I'm* not going anywhere. We have a lot to live for. Lupinites are made of tough stuff. Disease and injury don' keep us down for long."

Disease…

"That's right…this hospital, you chose it because you used to bring Finley here."

Bailey smiled bleakly. "Yes. St. Mercy knows how to treat Rioters. Moonchildren are safe here."

"How's she been?" Did Finley know about Maxwell yet? The thought of her reaction…

"Finley's been well. Dunno how I'm gonna break the news about Eddie. She's no stranger to hearing about our men dying, but this is her own mate, y'know? If I were in her shoes…I…I don' wanna think about it." His voice broke.

Sadiyeh didn't know how to respond. She turned to look out the window.

The clouds had parted slightly, showing a large full Moon, her dazzling light reflecting bright against the drenched city below. Bailey turned to study it.

"See that?" Bailey said. "A good sign, isn' it?"

Sadiyeh peered up at it.

"No matter what dey do to us, dey can' erase the Moon from the sky," Bailey said. "Nor da stars, nor da entire universe. Dey can cover our eyes for a bit with da clouds, but da Moonlight will always shine through. Don' matter if it's a New Moon night; the Moon is always there. Always put your faith in the Moon. She knows our pain. She knows all your secrets. Dat's what I always tell Finley. Put dat in your next book."

"Connor…" Sadiyeh said softly, turning toward Bailey. Her love rival who never was. She might have envied him, just a little, for having Gushiken all to himself, and he might have terrified her for a time, but she had never resented him.

Bailey had kept so much sorrow bottled up in his steel grey eyes, but the Moonlight exposed it all, so much so that it pained Sadiyeh to lock gazes with him. "Please, take care of Finley and Tetsu."

* * *

Thursday, September 4, 899 NE
Sadiyeh managed to catch up with Tora on her way to work that morning. The skies were overcast, grim and dark with the promise of more storms ahead.

"How's everyone?"

"Alive," Tora said. She wore Leon's jacket and sat hugging her knees. "Some were wounded, but overall they're faring better than Gushiken's men."

"How did you get there so quickly?"

"We happened to be by the pier when the gang attacked. We recognized Gushiken's car. We realized something had happened. We chased after them." She kept staring out over the empty grey skater park, lost in her thoughts. Sadiyeh debated whether to keep pressing her—she hated adding to Tora's bad mood—but something kept nagging at her.

"Did you get a good look at the gang?" Tora lived out on the streets. She surely would know all about the other gangs in the city.

"Yeah," Tora said, and her expression became unreadable. "I...I..."

And Tora left it at that.

* * *

Friday, September 5, 899 NE
"Hey, look at this."

Sadiyeh's eyes widened as she studied the recording framed in the tiny rectangular screen of Myskia's camera. There were Gushiken and his men; a tiny boy huddled off to the corner of the camera screen, barely visible; the other gang; and even some of the Nine Knives. The brawl, the transformation into wolves, the moment the mysterious gang cornered Gushiken, the brutal assault, the shots fired, the entire conflict—all caught on video camera.

"Where did you..."

"I heard people shouting, recognized some of the voices, saw the chase. I followed them. Luckily everything happened at the harbor. Wide, open space that allowed me to capture everything from high above. Managed to film the whole thing."

"Myskia! You recorded them?! You didn't even think to call the cops or—"

"What would the cops do? Arrest everyone, including

Gushiken? Or just the baddies because Gushiken's such a model citizen? Riot boss aside, you think cops act favorably toward Lupinites?" Myskia rolled their eyes. "Come on, Sadiyeh, think about it. This can be used in a court case, in our favor, should anything happen to Gushiken. And this is our history, in case…in case someday this is all that's left of us."

"Myskia…"

Myskia smiled ruefully. "Maybe I'm just being silly, but I've been thinking. What if someday we're no longer here? What if the United Domains have their way and the Moonchildren just fade out of existence? All the weirdo humans, gone! Forever! They're keeping us out of jobs, silencing us by not letting us tell our stories. We may be stifled, but at least this will survive. This video will be our voice, showing us fighting, struggling to survive. Sure, some will question its authenticity—let them try to prove it's doctored! I'd like to see them try!"

"So you chose to record a *fight*?! With *Rioters* at the center of it?!"

"Yes," Myskia said. "They can call us monsters, call us whatever the hell they want, but they made us into this—none of us would have turned to this lifestyle if not for the current state of the world. Let them see and let them know they had a hand in this."

Sadiyeh took a step back. The thought of Moonchildren no longer existing…

"Let's hope that never comes to pass," Sadiyeh said, her stomach twisting into knots.

Myskia snorted. "With the way things have been looking? That Lupinite family was all we had."

"Myskia, stop!" Sadiyeh didn't want to dwell on it. The past few nights, she had barely slept, unable to keep her thoughts from racing, worrying, wondering what the world would look like without Gushiken's Blue Moon Riot.

The Desmonite hopped onto the bridge's railing and leaned over, their expression turning somber. "I want to send this to Bailey, but I gotta admit I'm a bit nervous. You...you got a good look at that gang, right?"

Sadiyeh nodded slowly. She was starting to understand Tora's reaction earlier.

"Yeah..." Myskia glanced around nervously. "Don't know what the deal is with that...I don't know if I should make myself scarcer around the office from now on..."

The unease in Sadiyeh's stomach worsened. She had no proof, but Myskia's earlier words—*What if the United Domains have their way?*—echoed in the back of her head.

"Whatever makes you feel safe, Myskia."

* * *

Tuesday, September 9, 899 NE

Gushiken's condition didn't improve. He'd slipped into a coma, Bailey had informed Sadiyeh with an inscrutable expression. She couldn't even begin to imagine how he felt or what thoughts ran through his mind. She herself felt as though the entire world had stopped.

She wondered if silver had any detrimental effects on Lupinites, just as some legends of werewolves had claimed, but Bailey had assured her that no silver bullets had been used.

"We jus' need to wait it out," he said. "He may be healin'."

But how long will that take? Sadiyeh wondered. *Will he ever wake up?*

She hadn't written a single word since Gushiken had been hospitalized.

She had visited him from time to time, noting each time that some members of the Nine Knives gang were also there, presumably tasked by Bailey to guard Gushiken.

Bailey had taken over as the acting patriarch of the family. The shift barely made a change in how Iridium Bay Publishing operated, but nothing felt the same inside. The normal home-like atmosphere, despite the Riot office right next door, had disappeared, replaced with a thick, suffocating air of tension as everyone worked in silence, in fear of hearing news of Gushiken's death or of becoming the target of retaliation by the gang the Riot had fought.

Later that week, Maria wept to Sadiyeh about the state of affairs at the office. Where once the staff had grown so fond of Gushiken that they could lovingly—and lightly—tease their Riot overlord, no one dared to bring up his name now, for fear of enticing any sort of emotion from his husband, who was sure to fly off the handle at any moment. No one spoke, and no one dared to look Bailey in the eye.

"And if you think that's bad, I don't envy the other Rioters themselves," Maria had said. "Bailey's not hurting any of them, but goodness, imagine walking on eggshells around the husband of the patriarch! Russell and I have seen a few of them leaving the office with bruises or cuts on their faces."

"But you just said he's not hurting them!"

"Not intentionally. But I stopped one on the way out—played it off as just being nice and getting the first aid kit out, you know. They said Bailey's been having outbursts, and whenever he does, he starts throwing things. Sometimes it strikes one of his men. That's usually enough to knock him back to his senses. He feels horrible causing anyone pain, you know that. He's actually very sensitive."

Sadiyeh couldn't imagine what it was like being the recipient of one of those flying objects. She remembered how Bailey had circled her when she had first met him, giving the impression he was ready to slit her throat any moment, but she also thought back to how he had rescued her and taken down a human for groping her. She thought of his moment of gentleness when she was about to break down at the hospital, and the glimpses of fragility in his expression from time to time.

Strong. Insane. Wise. Vulnerable. That was Connor Bailey. But could he carry the weight of Blue Moon Riot on his shoulders?

* * *

Friday, September 19, 899 NE
One day, when Sadiyeh had stopped by the office for a brief visit, a window shattered, and the severed head of a wolf rolled right onto Maria's desk. Her terrified screams would reverberate in Sadiyeh's mind for days.

"No way…absolutely *not*!" Russell cried out. "That better not be a Lupinite's head!"

Everyone hushed as their heads snapped up to meet Bailey's stunned face. His fellow men flanked each side, but there was no word to describe the emotion that the Lupinite underboss tried to mask on his face.

Sadiyeh saw his fingers clench and his nails elongate into claws for a moment.

"Lowell," he growled at one of the younger Lupinites, a rookie by the looks of him. "Check for any note. Track them down."

The poor rookie stepped up and searched for the note, finding it lodged deep in the mouth of the disembodied head. He gave it a good sniff.

Sadiyeh slipped out wordlessly. She didn't wish to see any more.

* * *

More sleepless nights. The workdays dragged and bled into one another. Sadiyeh felt her mind grow numb and empty, like a television set without a signal. She spent her days staring at nothing, nowhere, zoning out, her fingers numb and cold to the touch.

She wished she could contact Midway, but she didn't wish to bother her. Her treatment was over. Midway had other patients to tend to, and Sadiyeh was older. She should be able to take better care of herself by now.

If only she could just *write*.

* * *

Saturday, September 27, NE

As much as Sadiyeh normally disliked being in public, she found the hospital a place of refuge. Gushiken's status hadn't changed ever since he had slipped into a coma, but Bailey was there frequently, and she knew some company was welcome.

She would sit wordlessly in Gushiken's room, staring at the pale blue walls, devoid of thoughts. Or she would sit out in one of the waiting rooms if Bailey needed time alone with Gushiken. Every now and again, the overhead would call an emergency code. She would see medical staff rush by, but as long as the code call wasn't for Gushiken's room, she could breathe a little easier. Just a little.

The nurses were content to leave her be. She wished one of them would notice that something was wrong with her.

One evening she spotted an Earthchild wearing large wooden bead bracelets reading one of her books in the waiting room. With a pang in her heart, she noted that the title was her very first publication with Iridium Bay Publishing.

"Is it any good?" she asked.

"Oh, yes," Bead Bracelet said. They smiled brightly. "I've been meaning to read it for some time. Glad I got around to it. It's helping keep my mind off my dad right now, you know."

Sadiyeh smiled through her pain. "I'm so glad it's brought you comfort."

The next thing Bead Bracelet said hit her right in the gut.

"Too bad this can't be a reality. Would have been cool, you know? Actually getting out there and exploring space."

Clenching her fist over her knees, Sadiyeh forced a smile.

"You never know! I mean, the discovery couldn't have been right, could it? We're learning something new every day. Got to keep an open mind!"

"I suppose," Bead Bracelet mused loudly, "but I mean, humans *did* used to believe ridiculous things before. They thought demons caused diseases, and then they thought vaccines made them sicker, can you believe that? Or that the world was flat—I mean, come on! They believed elves and ghosts existed. They believed all sorts of weird things because of ignorance, and if you asked them back then, they had all sorts of evidence ready to show you. It was the same in the prehistoric ages, and it was the same right before the Black Sun Era. Maybe that's why they had so many stories about space travel then, you know? Aliens were the new elves and angels of that time period. We were silly to get our hopes up."

Of course ghosts exist! Sadiyeh could barely keep herself from rolling her eyes. And elves could very well exist too, as well as aliens, and who even knew about angels. Of course, some of the old beliefs the Earthchild had stated were absurd, such as the world being flat, but the rationale the person used to justify a lack of space travel history was impossible to refute with her current state of mind.

This was the Cultural and Intellectual Reform at work. The seeds had been planted years ago, and she was powerless to stop it. After all, how could a tiny, silly, stupid little woman like her fight against such pragmatism?

What was it that Isaac Asimov wrote in one of his stories? Sadiyeh thought bitterly. *Something about being able to prove anything if one chooses the right postulate?*

She gave Bead Bracelet a nod, mentioned something about needing to be somewhere, and left.

They probably didn't mean anything bad, Sadiyeh told herself as she went and sat in a different waiting room on the opposite side of the hospital ward. *They just don't know, they just didn't know, everyone is being blindfolded, spiraling into the abyss—*

Alone and shaken, she conjured up Muse.

"I don't have any ideas to discuss with you," she said to them as they floated up like a tall ghostly curtain beside the window. "I just need someone to embrace. I'm trying to stay strong here for all my friends, but it's bringing back bad memories and fears of what may come. Everything's turning dark."

She slipped into their arms.

* * *

Leon tugged on Tora's arm. They had just passed Sadiyeh in the waiting room and seen her talking to someone before stepping into their arms.

"*Psst*, this is private!" he hissed, but Tora didn't budge. Cursing in Spanish, he tried again, but Tora just stood there, staring at Sadiyeh and Muse, dumfounded.

* * *

Thursday, October 2, 899 NE

After work, Sadiyeh stopped at a bookstore near the monorail station. Ever since the encounter with the Earthchild at the hospital, she couldn't stop wondering how else society had changed since her own admission to the hospital years prior, how else the United Domains were shaping the world. She wished to see for herself.

While she spotted books with names she was familiar with from Iridium Bay Publishing, she noted they were tucked away from plain view. A reader had to be specifically looking for the authors to find their work. It filled her with satisfaction that her books were among the widest read, displayed out in the open. The United Domains couldn't keep her books hidden. They couldn't silence her forever.

But for every book she had penned, dozens more existed to counter her voice. Books written with a lot more formality and in a style that filled her with envy. Books by far more learned individuals. Books by the acceptable, the privileged.

She spotted a bookshelf carrying works on astronomy, and she stopped to look around longingly. While information was still present, no books spoke of any of the Moon landings or space explorations of old. Those were just fairy tales now. The official consensus was that all scientific understanding of space came from telescopes alone. Outer space was untouchable.

As she turned away from that bookshelf, she heard two people, possibly Earthchildren, speaking animatedly.

"Excellent new edition, I'm telling you, a real eye-opener!"

"Does it say much about the people during the Black Sun Era?"

"Lots!"

Sadiyeh glanced their way, interest piqued, before the title hit her squarely in the face. *Our History in Blood.* Maria had ranted to her about that book during one of their dates.

"It argues that the reason why anyone survived the Black Sun Era was cannibalism," Sadiyeh piped up.

The Earthchild holding the book turned to Sadiyeh. "Of course," he said. "Makes sense, doesn't it? Nuclear winter, no vegetation for hundreds or thousands of years. The world had anywhere from five to twenty billion humans, possibly more, who knows, before it went dark. What happened to all of them?"

"The Floods had destroyed most of the major cities in the world! Multiple nuclear power plants had meltdowns, and no one could stop them—that's one of the reasons why we use Tiam technology instead nowadays! We were thrown into a digital dark age. We hadn't seen the Sun for ages, so we couldn't grow vegetation. It's a miracle any life survived at all!"

It was probably thanks, in part, to the Moonchildren, Sadiyeh thought.

"You're suggesting we turned violent with one another?" Sadiyeh went on. "That we're all descendants of those who would hurt others, and *that's* why our numbers decreased?"

The second Earthchild stopped to consider her words, but the one with the book just shook his head.

"They've done extensive research into our past," he said. "It wouldn't have been the first time humans got nasty with one another. What's the big deal, anyway? It's *fascinating*."

The big deal was...Sadiyeh had an uneasy feeling about all of this. She left in a huff.

* * *

Friday, October 3, 899 NE

"Your sister looks shaken up," Sadiyeh said to Russell, pulling him aside. Stopping by the office felt like a mistake after yesterday. Maria had barely noticed her.

"Can't blame her. Not with the company's future now in question."

Sadiyeh's throat went dry. "What do you mean?"

"No word on any improvement." Russell didn't need to say who he was talking about. "And everything's been in a state all week. I mean...if *he* goes...we're all thrown to the wolves, if you'll excuse the pun."

Sadiyeh didn't know how to reply to that. When she finally did speak, she kept her voice low. "You mean, if Gushiken... dies...Iridium Bay Publishing is over?"

"Well, think of it this way. The death of the patriarch leaves a power vacuum in the mob. You should know that."

"But Bailey is the acting patriarch!"

"And you think he's well enough to fight off anyone wanting to become the new leader of the pack?"

"They wouldn't—"

"Come on, Sadiyeh, you researched mobs of the past! There'll always be people looking to grab power for themselves!"

"But we're Moonchildren! We have to stick together!"

"We're still human! Humans have done dreadful things throughout history!"

The terrible feeling from her stomach crept up to her heart, wrapping around her like barbed vines. The claims that they were all descendants of cannibals...no answers beyond the stratosphere, no romanticized viewpoint of how the world had pulled itself out of the era of the Black Sun, no hope, no light or love…it didn't make sense. Had her recurring dreams been nonsense then? Figments of her imagination? Wishful thinking? "Oh, come on, Russell! Gushiken's men are loyal to him!"

"Yeah, and we thought the same about Adams, didn't we?"

The memory resurfaced. Gushiken loading the gun and firing it between Adam's eyes in practiced, mechanical movements. No love, no light…

She thought back to the bookstore, and the dread only grew colder inside her body. Cold, cold, *cold*…

* * *

Saturday, October 11, 899 NE

It was a dark and stormy night, like the night Sadiyeh had seen the Rioters carry away Gushiken.

She was having dinner, staring at the blank canvas across from her, when Brian approached her with a new letter from Amneh. She waited until she was in her bedroom to open it.

> *Dear Sadiyeh,*
> *Thank you so, so, so much for all your best wishes and prayers. In the end, I didn't get in. I don't know what I did wrong. I had met all the requirements for this school! My grades were high! I actually know how to spell now! I took extra classes and I had that really awesome teacher who helped me with grammar and everything!*
>
> *Whatever. I'm just going to put all my focus on finishing with top grades and see where life takes me after*

graduation. I don't need a degree to write anyway, right? You didn't either! I think I can get by okay without it. Still, I wish I could have gotten in.

Amneh Bamyeh

Sadiyeh set the letter down as something inside her began to splinter.

This couldn't be happening.

Sweet little Amneh. Sixteen years old. As bright as the Moon. Life had barely started, but obstacles already littered her path.

She drummed her fingers on her writing desk for a few moments before pulling her phone out. She composed a quick message to Maria. Sure, the future of Iridium Bay Publishing lay shrouded in uncertainty, but an internship was all Sadiyeh could offer Amneh. Whatever happened to the company after that, Amneh could at least find company in Sadiyeh's friends.

She set the phone aside and got to her feet. She paced across her bedroom, rubbing her hands together, trying to bring back some warmth into them.

They're barring us from universities now, Sadiyeh thought. *They're silencing us even more!*

Was that all part of the Cultural and Intellectual Reform? Silence the Moonchildren so that their frivolous talks of blood purification, shape-shifting into wolves, and magic would not reach the ears of the rest of the human population? Block them from opportunities the moment they left high school so they could not progress into the real world?

The harder she thought, the bleaker the future appeared. Slowly, Moonchildren would be denied entry to schools and colleges. Not good enough. Just try harder. Almost had it! They would be left behind as the rest of the human world flourished, left to continue swallowing strange shallow truths espoused by the privileged elite.

Where would they go? What would happen to them?

Could they continue to rely on the society built and provided by the criminal underworld, always living on the outskirts of the law? Would Lupinite Riots be able to help everyone? Look how easily *this* one had fallen apart! The patriarch was on his deathbed while others lurked in the shadows, ready to ambush Bailey for a chance to become the new leader. The family would splinter. Resentments would fester. It wasn't going to remain peaceful...

Gripping the back of her chair, Sadiyeh glanced about. Murklins Manor, her home, such a wonderful place to just sit and hide away forever. But while she had a sanctuary, what about everyone else? All of her friends, Amneh's family, the entire Blue Moon Riot, every Moonchild in danger now and forever? Where could they hide?

And what use was a comfortable home if she could not *live*? What use was a home if she could not ever publish again? To exist, but not live?

Panic set in.

I'm just one of the undead, aren't I?

Nowhere left to run.

She just wanted to write. All she ever wanted was to tell stories, not to feel so cold, empty, broken.

She took her prized pen off the table and pressed it, waiting patiently as Muse issued from the tip and stood hovering above her.

The ever so loyal Muse. She almost wept before them as she fell onto her writing chair.

"I'm not feeling well," Sadiyeh said. "I want to escape this world. I just want to write. I haven't been able to for over a month. I know that sounds silly, but it's hurting me. I can't think straight. I've been crying constantly. I'm worried for so many people, for what the future holds. I wish I could run away. I just want to get out of here for some time…"

Muse studied her silently for a few seconds. Then they swept closer and pressed their forehead against hers.

* * *

Sadiyeh stayed in her room and wrote all through Saturday night and well into the following day. By the time she emerged from her bedroom, shaking from hunger, she could barely finish a small cup of soup before the itch to write consumed her once more.

"I do not mean to get in the way of your work, Ms. Mhalabiyeh," Brian said, "but shouldn't you be preparing for work tomorrow?"

Work. Without a thought—was she insane for doing this?—Sadiyeh grabbed her phone and sent a quick message to her boss at the lab, informing him that she would no longer be coming in to work.

With her job no longer an issue, Sadiyeh wrote all through the night, Muse loyally by her side the entire time.

The next day went the same, as did the day after that, and the day after that. Brian had inquired about her presence at home, but Sadiyeh brushed him off.

"Don't interrupt me," she had said. "I don't want to lose my train of thought!"

By the end of the week, Sadiyeh had barely made an appearance at the dining table. Brian had resorted to leaving trays of food by her bedroom door. Most went uneaten.

"You'll enjoy your meals so much more if you come sit down with us," he cajoled.

"I'm fine like this, thank you," came Sadiyeh's faint reply from within. "I'm busy. Please don't disturb me."

"I'll never understand artists," Brian muttered before walking away.

* * *

Over the course of the next few months, Sadiyeh Mhalabiyeh wrote her greatest works.

She seldom slept. Seldom ate. Seldom left her room.

Any lingering conversations with her friends tapered away, as she did not even reply to a text message or email.

Sometimes the walls would cave in, and Sadiyeh could feel barbed vines enclosing her. Muse would find her clutching her knees, huddled in a corner, whimpering, her eyes large and unseeing, before she would compose herself and fill her mind with distractions: her world, her many worlds, her many realities that were far kinder than the crumbling one beyond her window.

At the comfort of her desk, she wrote with creative abandon. At her desk, she withered away, while Muse silently watched.

She didn't know where or how she got all this sudden creative drive and energy. The thirst to keep writing kept her at her desk, her fingers flying over the keyboard or scribbling away madly in her notebook. The pile of manuscripts rose higher and higher next to her.

She revisited old drafts and woke up with new ideas. She found the words for many of the series she had left hanging, such as *Through Thick and Gin* and *Mastika Milk*, the latter inspired by the Nine Knives. She penned new novels, including a thick book titled *Suzuki Taxi* about an intergalactic crime-fighting detective android; *Ride the Spiral*, a curious, mystery-riddled book dedicated to Maria, with a morally complex protagonist she was sure Maria would enjoy; and *Foster the Monster* to tickle Franklin and the rest of the Manor residents.

The final book in the *Branded Trilogy*, which she had initially wished to title *Branded to Death*, was renamed *Branded on Moonlight* and given a far more optimistic conclusion.

The *These Nuts May Vary* series got two new additions: *Stewpots for Robots* and *Berries for Fairies*. The *Bad Birds Trilogy* got what would become its highest-selling installment of all time, *Loot of the Pirate Parrots*, for reasons Sadiyeh would never come to find out. While she wrote that particular book, Sadiyeh's chuckles could be heard outside her bedroom—a rare sound indeed.

The residents of the manor would often stop by her door and stare in silent worry. How many weeks had it been now? How many months? Was this normal for her? They knew not to disturb her—she could be a real witch when her creative thoughts were rudely interrupted—but how long was this going to last?

When was the last time Sadiyeh had left the house?

When was the last time anyone had seen her?

* * *

New Year's Eve, 899 NE
Maria frowned at her phone, unable to enjoy the annual end-of-year office party going on around her, considerably smaller and quieter than those of previous years. She had done as Sadiyeh had requested, had written a glowing letter of recommendation for Amneh Al-Ghul—not that the brilliant young woman needed it. Gushiken and Bailey would hire her solely for being a Moonchild, and especially for being Sadiyeh's cousin. This was simply a formality.

But what concerned Maria most right now was Sadiyeh. She hadn't returned any of Maria's messages or emails. Hadn't picked up the notes on her latest manuscript either. She *had* mentioned getting an idea for a book and needing time to write, but then…nothing.

"She's done disappearing acts before," Russell said.

"Not for this long," Maria said. "She'd usually pop in every now and then for lunch. I don't care how focused you are on your creative work! You can't be doing it night and day! It's impossible! The mind needs time to recuperate, you know? She understands that!"

Checking her phone again—*Where are you? I miss you!*—she

gave a heavy sigh and tossed it next to her on the couch. "If something—Moon Mother forbid!—has happened to her, we'd have known by now, right? Right?"

"Yeah," Russell said as he shifted his weight, looking around uncomfortably. "Yeah…"

* * *

"Really?! I need that back *now*!"

"It wasn't me, Fahad!"

"I know it was you, Duma!"

"Duma? I think Bobbie meant Puma!" Puma shrieked as she skated by, Fahad's keys and pocketknife in her hand.

"Puma! Get back here!"

Lynx just rolled their eyes and stuck their face closer to the laptop screen. Agu chuckled and leaned back on the big torn-up couch next to them, watching the chaos.

That was the scene Leon witnessed as he passed them by. The whole place was a mess, but Leon's main concern was someone beyond their little hideout.

He stepped out to find Tora lying flat on her back atop an abandoned car. It must have been red back in the day but was now layered in rust, tire-less, and covered in snow. Tora was gazing up at the Moon, its light accentuating her pensive frown.

"I can't stop thinking about what we saw that evening," Tora said as Leon joined her.

"Which night would that be?" Leon snickered. They saw a whole lot of shit every night. "The gang or—"

"Sadiyeh. That…thing at the hospital. She conjured it up."

"What about it?"

Tora made a little pout as if struggling to find the right words. "Magic…doesn't work like that."

"Uh…what'd you mean?"

"Magic is more…external, I suppose? Think of it like this: The world, the whole universe, is a long tapestry stretched out on a loom. Magi have powers that allow them to shift threads on that loom, be it a single thread or several, depending on their individual strength. They cannot change the entire loom, of course, because they are not omnipotent. No Magi is that powerful.

"Magic can be split into three main categories: healing, aiding, and warding, and those three can each be further split into three categories each. Magi can divine. They can be highly attuned to their surroundings, they can derive medicinal properties from the world around them, they can perform little magics to make life more convenient for themselves. They have just enough power to make small changes to better their lives and others.

"Sadiyeh's power is different. It's more internal. She's conjured something from inside herself. She can create entire looms and manipulate them, like the entire world is her oyster, instead of her struggling to work with the universe around her. The ease with which she conjured that being…that's not what Magi are. That's something beyond. I've seen this before, a long time ago. It's strange. What could this mean?"

Leon's eyebrows furrowed. *What in the freshly baked fuck?!* He sat up and stared at Tora as if seeing her for the very first time.

"T...how the *hell* do you know so much about this?"
Tora's eyes widened. "U-um, well..."

* * *

Connor Bailey kissed Tetsu's temple after helping him back onto the bed.

"Yer ole strength is returning, love," he said. "Keep dis up and ya'll be able to take out da ringleader yerself in no time. Consider it a gift from me to ya."

Tetsu gave a snort and a short laugh. He had woken up from his coma about a month ago, but there was still much recovering to do. His body healed faster than a non-Lupinite's would, though, and he was finally back home, finally back with his Connor, with the instructions left by his therapist, and a fire burning in his chest.

He reached out and brushed his thumb under Connor's eye over the scar, which curled over his sharp cheekbone. "One of his men did this to you, love?"

"Eh, it's nothing. Got a bit carried away an' wanted to get a bit of revenge for ya."

"And almost died trying, by the looks of it. Don't leave me, love."

"Never would dream of it. 'Fraid ya're forever stuck with me."

Tetsu's face stretched in a grin. "Absolute bastard. This is why I fell for you." He jerked suddenly, pain shooting through his side.

"Easy! Anyone else woulda died on the spot from injuries like yers," Connor said.

Resolved to remain in bed, Tetsu stared at the high ceiling of their bedroom for a few moments, while his husband busied about the room before breaking the silence.

"Those men we fought…"

"Aye, just concentrate on healing."

"Garrett informed me that Myskia has a recording of the whole ordeal."

Connor looked up. "Dey do."

"I wish to review it," Connor said. "Something about those men…"

His face set in a frown as he recalled back that day.

"Oh! The pup. Are you still watching over him?"

"Like he was one of my own. He's been stayin' with Finley while I patched ya up."

"Bring him over."

"Aye, love."

Connor left for a couple of hours. When he returned, he was clutching the hand of a small child with dark curly hair and large dark eyes. The tiny, shy boy held a soft plush dragon to his chest. His eyes darted around the room, scanning for danger, but once they landed on Tetsu, they widened, and a gasp escaped his mouth.

"D'ya know who dis is?" Connor asked, laying a gentle hand on the boy's shoulder.

"My hero!" the boy squeaked.

Tetsu chuckled.

The boy bowed, both his forehead and the dragon's touching the carpeted floor. "I'm sorry I caused you trouble, sir!"

"It was an honor to protect you," Tetsu said. "What is your name, dear little boy?"

"Ali, sir! Ali Alamar!"

"Ali. Wonderful to meet you." The smile faded as Tetsu turned to Connor. "Alamar? His father wasn't—"

"'Fraid he was," Connor said. "We checked on his clinic shortly after da pup told us who he was. Da place was ransacked."

"And you suspect it was by the same people we fought?"

"Can' imagine it being anyone else."

"But Connor…why would a group of Desmonites target a Mooncousin?"

Connor shrugged his shoulders. "Dey didn' give us any reason."

"You sent our allies to investigate?"

"Found nothin'."

Tetsu rubbed his chin as he studied the little boy holding onto his plush toy. He had connections with Dr. Alamar. Could the gang have been targeting him all this time?

"This won't do…won't do at all," he said in a low voice. "We must remain united during this time. We'll locate the gang and approach them diplomatically. Perhaps we can achieve an alliance."

"And what if dey're not interested in any of dat?"

"Then we'll kill them." He did not look at Ali when he said those words. "We can't endanger the rest of the people we are protecting."

Connor gave a nod. Ali buried his face in the dragon.

Adorable, Tetsu thought. He was going to have to ask another favor from Connor regarding the pup. A long-term commitment, as he could not overwhelm Finley with another child to look after. And he did owe Dr. Alamar for having helped the family for many years.

"What of the rest of our pack?" Tetsu asked. "The Riot doing well? Our clients? Anyone gone missing? Anyone in danger or dead?"

Connor shook his head. "Nothin' recently. To be honest, I've jus' been too busy."

"Is Sadiyeh all right? I know these matters tend to affect her deeply."

Connor's mouth fell open, then closed, and then opened again. He looked almost comical as he tried to recall something.

"Ya know…I don' think I've seen or heard from Sadiyeh in a while."

Tetsu's brow set into a frown. "Oh? When was the last time you spoke with her?"

"I…I dunno," Connor said. "While ya were still at the hospital? Shit, I've been so busy with everything, tryin' to keep the family together, protectin' the businesses, I…"

Tetsu struggled to lean forward again. "Get someone to check in on her. I don't have a good feeling about this."

* * *

New Year's Day, 900 NE

The resemblance was so uncanny that AC-A893, formerly known as Midway, stopped and stared at the young woman just to make sure that it wasn't Sadiyeh herself.

She had the same brilliant blue eyes, but her dark hair was shorter, very thick, and curly; it was pulled away from her face in a low ponytail. A swath of baby hairs curled around her hairline.

The woman appeared younger than Sadiyeh, and AC-A893 wondered if this was the cousin Sadiyeh had so often spoken of: Amneh Al-Ghul, or Amneh Bamyeh, as she signed her letters. She was walking about the station early this morning with uncertain steps, a newcomer, stopping to check a billboard every so often.

AC-A893 was about to go—she had no business interacting with this possible Amneh—when the girl spotted her.

"Oh! You're looking at me! Do you know me, android?"

AC-A893 froze on the spot as the girl ran up to her. "My cousin mentioned someone like you. Are you Midway?"

"Patient confidentiality. I cannot confirm nor deny whether any of my patients have addressed me by such a name."

Amneh blew air heavily through her teeth. "Well, that's inconvenient! I was supposed to meet with some people my cousin set me up with later this week, but I decided to stop by sooner. I mean, I just don't know the area! And like hell I'm gonna ask my dad to help! 'Why don't you just get married?' What, you think just because I didn't get into college that's all I'm bleeding good for?! And like, sure, I'd like to get married *some*day—someone big and powerful, like a Rioter—but not right now, *goodness*!"

AC-A893 only stared and nodded.

"You sure you don't know Sadiyeh? You'd have just walked away by now. Other androids usually do." Amneh narrowed her eyes.

AC-A893 struggled for a response. "I have already informed you, per protocols, we cannot disclose any information about our patients without their informed consent."

"But you *do* work in the health field!" Amneh pointed out. "I hope you have some information to give me! Sadiyeh's not been in contact with me for a while now. Even when she's nose deep in a new project, she at least sends a sticker reaction to my messages!"

Something flipped on inside AC-A893, the part in all androids built to ensure the safety of humans. But would this compromise Sadiyeh's trust in her?

Just then, a short middle-aged man with greying hair and glasses approached them.

"Did you just say Sadiyeh?" he asked. "Apologies, but you look so much like my employee."

Amneh stopped and stared at him in confusion. The man had his white coat thrown over his briefcase, but his name was still visible on the breast pocket: Dr. Ernesto Fernandez.

"My cousin works for you?" Amneh asked.

"Well, *worked* for is more like it," Dr. Fernandez said. "She sent me a text out of the blue back in October. Let me double-check…yes, October 12."

Not since October 12? AC-A893 thought. Two months, twenty days…On the surface, it wasn't so alarming. Sadiyeh had her moments of shutting herself in to write—

"Just up and quit her job. Never heard from her since."

—but she had never quit her job or lost contact with all of her friends!

"That's not like her at all!" AC-A893 gasped.

Amneh rounded on her and shrieked, "So you *do* know her!"

A large wolf rushed over to them, huffing madly. Undeterred at being seen by a bunch of shocked onlookers, the wolf morphed back into a sharply dressed human man.

"Sorry to frighten you," the Lupinite said. "Thought you were Sadiyeh."

"Everyone says that," Amneh said in a huff, "but no one can tell me where she is. I have to get to her! I must see her! I have a bad feeling about all of this!"

"The name's Charles Lowell," the Lupinite said, "and we've been looking as well. Boss's orders. No one even knows where she lives."

AC-A893 frowned. Why was everyone so eager to locate Sadiyeh? What had happened?

"You're looking for her *too*?" Amneh asked.

"Please," Lowell said with a bow. "Our boss was gravely wounded. It must have impacted Ms. Sadiyeh deeply—"

Oh, no. AC-A893's eyes widened. Sadiyeh had been doing so well—

"We fear that's the reason why she's gone silent. I could have sworn her friend Maria would know where Sadiyeh lives. Do any of you know of a Maria Vine? I cannot seem to locate her—"

Midway stepped forward. "I can show you the way to her house."

* * *

Earlier, on the cusp of the new year, 900 NE
With a strange sense of bittersweetness, Sadiyeh set aside her twelfth manuscript, now complete. This one was her largest yet. Her magnum opus, inspired by a series of odd recurring dreams that began when she was a little girl. The story had

changed throughout the years and kept growing. The entire work must have been well over three million words by now. It would best be split into multiple volumes, as Sadiyeh indicated in a note for Maria to read later.

From her window she saw it was a snowy winter night, graced with a beautiful full Moon. A bone-deep feeling of fatigue was beginning to set in, but she fought against it. There was one more story she had to write. Just one more.

And this one was going to be very special.

It had taken her many years, but she had finally found the words to the storybook she had promised to write for Amneh. She could not draw the illustrations herself, but that would probably be Russell's job. For now, she would write.

She grabbed some paper, sketched out a couple of scenes, and slipped back into the zone, with Muse, as always, hovering by her side.

As she penned the final word, the clock struck midnight, heralding the new year. Her prized pen slipped out of her fingers and rolled onto the ground. Sadiyeh dropped her head forward and shut her eyes. Muse watched silently, silently, silently, until they too faded into the morning.

Chapter 5

Once upon a Time

FOREWORD FROM THE EDITOR:

My cousin, the celebrated author Sadiyeh Mhalabiyeh, passed away on the morning of January 1, 900 NE, sixty-four years ago this year. That morning is still seared into my memory. Even as I sit here typing this, so much older, the memory of that day comes back to me vividly, raw and painful. Although Sadiyeh had battled a darkness for half her time on Earth, she never meant to end her life on that night. That much was clear from the notes she left on her manuscripts. She was looking forward to discussing all the stories she had fervently produced in that short amount of time.

She had holed herself away so she could escape, because she felt there was nowhere else to hide from a world that had become cold and cruel to those like her. She felt cornered, and her writing was all that comforted her. The laws passed by our leaders made her feel this way.

She left us over a dozen new works, which I and my coeditor, the late Maria Vine, have released over the years. I thank every one of you who have sent letters to our company. Your words mean so much to us.

You are holding Sadiyeh's forty-second and final book. Vine and I both believe this book was meant to be read last: a storybook she had written to fulfill a promise to me. Thus we have saved it for what would have been my dear Sadiyeh's one hundredth birthday.

Although this book was written with me in mind, I do not believe it is solely dedicated to me. It belongs to the countless others Sadiyeh knew and loved, many of whom have long since passed by the time of this publication.

The language and tone are a little more adult, a little darker in theme than your typical children's picture book, hence this foreword. I am certain not many higher-ups would be pleased with its existence, but we have decided to publish this book, for we feel Sadiyeh wished to impart a final message to the entire world. As for what that message is, I will let you, the reader, decide.

Please be good to yourself and others. Be well, and be kind.
—Amneh Bamyeh, 964 NE

DELIVERANCE IN THE DARK

EVERY WORM HAS A STORY TO TELL
By Sadiyeh Mhalabiyeh
Edited by Amneh Bamyeh and Maria Vine (†)
Iridium Bay Publishing
© 964 NE

Once upon a time, rain poured down from cloudy skies
and a downpour came down on Old Towne till sunrise.

Soil, tree, and grass stood glossy with dew,
and high above birds sang and flew.

On the sidewalks were worms that wiggled.
They looked like ugly little red squiggles!

There was a little boy named Dom who loved the outdoors
He counted to the moment he could leave his home—
How he grew sick of playing with his dinosaurs!

Little Dom ran out whooping, a spring in his step,
and he did stop to see what he killed at his doorstep.

"Joy! Joy!" called Dom for his friend. "The sun is shining!"
"There are worms!" cried little Joy from her house. "I'm not coming out!"
Replied Dom, "Then come stomp with me and quit your whining!"

L. M. BLADE

Little Joy stepped out of her house, small and shy.
She was terrified of the worms. She couldn't even say why.

They didn't look like tiny snakes, because they didn't have rattles on their tails;
They couldn't bite you or kill you or chase after you.
But one look and she'd go running back home feeling ill and frail!

Dom saw the look on Joy's face. He stomped on a worm before her eyes.
"See? They're helpless! They won't do anything! Stomp with me!" said Dom.
And he went about, taking every worm in his path by surprise.

Little Joy wove between the worms, afraid to step on a single one.
She grew frustrated; she just wanted to have some fun!

"What are you waiting for?" cried Dom.
"Pretend you're at war!"

"They're ugly and scary!" cried back Joy. She'd much rather be back home hugging her puppy Cherry!

DELIVERANCE IN THE DARK

Dom left her and went on his rampage, and every worm met its death by a stomp.
Joy was left all alone, listening to sounds of *whomp, whomp, whomp*.

"Maybe Dom is right," said Joy while Dom was far away.
"I cannot play if the worms are in my way!"

Joy found a worm squirming on the ground.
She raised her foot, then thought she heard a sound.

"Dom, is that you?"
But Dom was far from view.

Joy looked down to the worm and realized it was scared.
"Did you make the sound?" asked Joy as she stared.

"That terrible boy," said the worm, "he killed my friend."
"Friend?" asked Joy. Worms had friends? And this worm could not defend his friend, how terrible!

"I'm sorry!" said Joy. "It was raining, and my friend Dom—you've seen him around—doesn't like the idea of anything or anyone in his path. Why did you come up from the ground?"

L. M. BLADE

"We lost our homes in the Floods," explained the worm. "We cannot breathe when it rains. Water fills our little lungs!"

"How awful!" said Joy.

"We do not mean to cause trouble," said the worm. "Once it's dry, we'll return home right on the double.

"Your friend is cruel. He treats us like pests, stomping on us although we're your underground guests!"

"I'm sorry," said Joy. "I'll speak with Dom, and hope I can knock some sense into him, and if that fails, I'll tell his mom!"

"Do that. We wish you luck," said the worms. "Doesn't change the fact:
our homes are gone, we're stuck out here, and we're under attack."

"What were you doing before you came up?" asked Joy.

"I was on my way to school," said the tiniest worm. "All the things I could learn!
But then my class became a pool, and my whole day took a downturn."

DELIVERANCE IN THE DARK

"I am a doctor," said a worm with impatience, "and
I don't mean to be a cynic,
but how do you expect me to take care of my
patients without a clinic?!"

"All I wanted was to make art," said another. "I
had works that now I'll never impart,
For my studio is flooded, all my creations are
gone, and my heart is falling apart!"

Said another, "I just want to find my mother.
My sister got lost in the twister,
and I'm worried my brother is smothered by your
friend."

"I just came out here to protect," said a large
worm, voice full of authority.
"Worms find their friends and family through me to
reconnect,
And maintaining the dignity of my kin is my priority
For I sniff out all wrongs to right and correct."

More worms chimed in, more worms told Joy their story.
Tales of pain and toil and suffering, and of the glory.
And Joy sat and listened as if fixed by a spell.
Every worm had a story to tell!

L. M. BLADE

Joy began to cry; her tears hit the ground like tiny rain.
"Please dry your eyes!" said the worms. "We did
not mean to cause you pain!

"We are used to this. We know how to adapt.
We only request of you: don't kill us when we're
trapped!"

Joy searched for Dom far and near
to put an end to his cruel game,
because worms were not so different from you and me;
we are all one and the same.

Joy wept because she was scared.
Dom could come and kill all her friends,
leaving not one worm spared,
before she got to make any amends.

Worms belong here. They are part of this world
as much as she, he, you, and me.
We are all part of this world.

She wept as grief overtook her, but she should not
despair,
and neither should you, oh reader with whom this
story I share.

DELIVERANCE IN THE DARK

Dark days may come ahead that will fill you with dread.
Do not despair. Do not let darkness win.
You'll one day learn all of existence is of one kin.
So hold on to hope, look to the stars,
and hold on to your elders' memoirs.

Protect your fellows as friends and family. Don't fret; it'll be all right,
for everything in existence is made of love, life, and Moonlight.

Made in the USA
Columbia, SC
02 June 2022